GIRLS' TIME

A PSYCHOLOGICAL THRILLER

GIRLS' TRILOGY BOOK 3

JASON LETTS

COPYRIGHT & DISCLAIMER

1
_____

Mom's aim is as bad as her parenting.

When the gun goes off, I'm already half turned away and ducking in the vain hope that a bullet to the shoulder would be survivable. Truth be told, I'd rather not be shot anywhere. I mean, the human body already has enough holes.

I don't know where the bullet goes, because my eyes are shut tight, but I don't waste any time acting as though it got me. Flopping flat against the floor without anything to stop my fall, since my hands are still cuffed behind my back, brings another wave of pain, but it can't be anywhere near as bad as actually being shot.

The thing that hurts the most is that it's my parents who are doing this to me. After living on my own on the streets for five years, I thought I had become so tough that they couldn't hurt me, but what they said easily cut through my thick skin.

I thought they didn't care about me and didn't want to be around me. I was fine with that. I had no idea how much they hated me and felt personally justified having me killed or doing it themselves if there was a chance I would get in the way of their vicious investment scheme.

And then there's what they did to my little sister, Melanie, the sweetest, most innocent girl in the world...

"Alright, let's get going. We're done here," Diedre says, presumably still behind the desk where she had gotten her dainty little pistol.

I don't need to see her face to tell she has no remorse for what she's done. The tone of her voice says it all, the decisiveness, the matter-of-factness. She sounds like she could actually make a good CEO conducting herself like that, except it's too bad she built an entire company to scam investors through Bedrock Financial's Q Fund, a Ponzi scheme.

And now they've stolen all of the fund's money during a fake FBI raid and are about to make a run for it.

All I can do while the whole bruised side of my face is mashed into the floor is try to act dead, keeping as still as I can even though my heart is pounding and I want to gasp for breath.

But if I take more than the shallowest breath or twitch a finger, I know she'll fire another shot standing right over me, one that won't miss. As it is, I can only hope they think I've fallen on my wound and any blood from the gunshot is pooling underneath me.

I hear signs of some movement, and I guess my mom is grabbing her bag and getting ready to get out of here. Listening intently like this makes me realize how bone-tired I am after everything I've been through. It's almost enough to make me think I am actually dead.

"Don't you think we should do something?" my dad, Marty Marks, says in his smooth, rich voice.

I think he's suggesting they should do something for me. Yes, I need help, and I would be more than happy if they had a change of heart and started to provide some. It sounds like a long shot, but I imagine them helping me up and getting me some medical attention. If it takes shooting at me for them to realize they care at least a tiny bit, it might actually be worth it.

A scoff fills the room.

"Are you kidding me? Ew, gross. I don't even want to look at her like that. Did you know that the body voids its bowels when it dies? I've wiped her bottom enough times and don't want to be anywhere around that ever again."

Apparently my mother is more used to my father's charms than I am. She isn't swayed in the slightest.

My dad sighs.

"No, I wouldn't either, but—"

"I know that!" Mom interrupts, chuckling. "I don't think you've ever touched a diaper in your life."

"That's because you were always so good at changing them. But that's not what I'm getting at. Shouldn't we do something to get rid of her body?"

My vain hope that my father was actually advocating for my behalf falls to pieces, though I probably shouldn't be surprised. He stood by while my mom was shooting at me, helping her take the safety off. It takes all of my willpower to keep from snarling.

So still, shallow breaths.

"What's the point?" Diedre says shrilly. "We're never coming back here, and no one's ever going to find us. Whoever shows up here can deal with her however they like, for all I care. I'd imagine some police officer or detective will do something. It's the least they can do after everything we've paid in taxes."

A distinct pause follows before raucous laughter erupts from the two of them. Like they paid any taxes.

Considering their behavior before they attempted to end my life, I can only imagine they're falling all over each other with unrestrained amusement and affectionate touches only a short distance from where they believe my dead body to be.

"You're right though. It's high time we get out of this dump. I know it's going to be busy traveling, but we should find time to celebrate," he says suggestively, making me sick.

I can hear some more movement and have to think they're only a few feet away and heading past me in the direction of the door.

"Uh-huh, is that so? Funny how you're in the mood to celebrate like this pretty much every day. But it is going to be a relief to finally get out of here. Can you imagine five years locked up in this penthouse? I'm going to frolic and run and feel the wind in my hair again," she says, her excitement making her sound younger, more the way I remember.

As they're walking past, I'm already starting to wonder if I'm in the clear. The way they're talking makes it seem like they've forgotten me completely. Even after all of the callous, heartless things they've both said and done, I'm still astonished that there isn't even the tiniest ounce of guilt or misgivings in their heads.

I hear the click of the door opening and suppose that's it. They're going to simply walk out and leave me like this without so much as a second thought. As much as I bitterly remember so much of what they did to Melanie and me, I still had some warm memories and wouldn't leave them dead on the floor.

"After you," Marty says, holding the door open.

I expect to hear a few more footsteps before the door closes, leaving me completely alone, but instead there's nothing.

Straining my ears makes me think I've somehow missed them walking out. Are they already gone? With my eyes shut and the shallow breathing, on top of all of the aches and pains, I feel like I'm fading out. This floor is not soft at all, but I feel like I'm glued to it and couldn't get up if I wanted to.

"No, wait. This isn't right," Mom says, and I nearly blink and jerk at the recognition that they're still here. "I won't be able to live with myself if we leave like this."

And to my surprise it sounds like my mom might be recognizing that this is actually deeply, terribly wrong.

Some footsteps follow, and I have to keep from tensing up at the prospect of my mother coming over to check on me. But then I notice the footsteps aren't coming in my direction. The squeak of a hinge follows, some faint clattering, and then more footsteps.

"Can you believe I almost forgot these? Diamonds are a girl's best friend. Come on. I'm starting to notice the smell in here from her already. While she's six feet underground, these will sparkle brilliantly on the beach."

I hear the door closing and latch shut, my dad's voice barely audible on the other side.

"The next step in your plan means we can't lounge all the time though. Poor Emily. If she thought this was all about stealing a bunch of money, she was sorely mistaken."

2

I've had some sad walks of shame in my life, but this has to be the most pathetic.

When my eyes open, I see through the large office window that it's the crack of dawn and know immediately that I have to get out of the Bedrock building. I suppose now I should be thankful that my parents left for good, because if they'd forgotten something and come back they probably would've finished what they started with me.

Groaning, I realize it's not a good sign that I'm in such a wretched condition that I've passed out on the floor. The dried beer on me smells even more pungent. Then there's the dust, the dirty tank top, the small picture frame in my pocket digging into my thigh, the bonus check to Alice, and my countless injuries.

And I can't forget about the handcuffs chafing my wrists behind my back, though now that I have a moment to myself I can do something about them. It takes some work sliding them over my hips and working my legs through, but finally I can get my hands in front of me, at the cost of some pins and needles as the blood flow resumes.

In no time at all, I'm confronted with what I have to do. My parents have left but need to be tracked down to pay for their scam and what they did to me. I have to get out of this building without anyone seeing me, especially since I trashed the human resources office. And I need to find my sister, my guiding light, to find out what happened to her.

If there's one person who might have an idea what my parents are up to, it's Melanie.

I lurch to my feet, enduring another wave of discomfort from my ankle and hip, and start to get moving. Even ransacking this room seems like too big of a risk when some other executive could show up for work early, catch me, and tip off Mom and Dad that I'm still alive.

The rich furnishings of the penthouse apartment up here on the top floor get up my ire as I trudge back to the elevator. This is the luxurious life my mother lived for five years while I was homeless and couch surfing through Dallas and Melanie was behind bars.

The vacant hallway leads to an empty elevator, dinging as though everything is normal and taking me down to the ground floor. No one's here yet, and I'm thankfully able to slip out through the doors without being seen.

But being out on the streets is a different matter, and I'm not in any kind of place where I can rest yet. Morning traffic is starting up, and early risers are starting to appear on the streets. They're treated to the sight of me hobbling along the sidewalk with handcuffs on looking like I've been through a tornado.

The logical thing to do would be to find a way to get to my apartment or Alice's, but that wouldn't help me with my current problem and could very well deliver me into the arms of the police or my parents' FBI agent imposters.

It strikes me that this whole "looking like I'm running from the cops" style isn't doing me any favors, and even trying to twist or cross my arms isn't enough to hide the handcuffs. I need a solution for this, fast.

If only I had a phone on me, this would be a lot easier. Maybe I was a bit hasty tossing Alice's phone into the trash after talking to the McCurtain County sheriff. For some reason they consider me a person of interest in their investigation and want to see me immediately. It probably has something to do with how I killed her and then assumed her identity, but who can be sure?

My slinking around the city in the first rays of daylight goes on long enough for me to find a solution, a hardware store with workmen streaming in and out prior to starting their jobs for the day. I'm under no illusion that I could buy some sort of tool to get me out of these cuffs, but I'm hopeful that I can give someone a good reason to help me.

Inside, there's a middle-aged man with a full beard, hairy forearms, and a thick mane who sees me enter. I limp over awkwardly, my hair a mess and tank top showing more of my chest than I would like, handcuffs in plain view.

I can't imagine what he must be thinking. Actually, scratch that. I can easily imagine what he's thinking.

I raise my hands, the cuffs clinking a little, and conjure a shy smile.

"Hi, can you help? My boyfriend lost the key," I say with a straight face and watch as the guy's head explodes.

"Uh, sure," he stammers, leaping into action once his circuits aren't so fried.

He takes me over to a section where there are some bolt cutters on the wall and makes short work of the handcuffs, which drop to the floor with a satisfying clatter. And it goes without saying that he's being paid for his service in entertainment value, not money.

"Thank you," I say, rubbing my wrists and giving him

another innocent look. "Do you happen to have any ointment that can help with whip burn?"

He shakes his head, eyes wide and mouth agape, and I leave him with a story to tell for the rest of his life.

Once I'm back on the street and reveling in the unfettered use of my arms, my ruse reminds me of my kind-of boyfriend, Miles. He doesn't realize he's my boyfriend yet, but we'll keep working on that, and the kiss we shared when the police were dragging me away should've gone a long way to settling the matter. But I sense he's the kind of guy who prefers things to be spelled out.

Gray areas, ambiguity, and anything less than the full truth are not his style.

It might have something to do with how he's honest and seems to care about doing the right thing, which puts him at odds with almost everyone I've ever known my entire life.

Too bad I only met him yesterday and have no idea what his phone number is or where he lives. Even his last name is a blank. He deduced that my parents were running a massive scam through their company, and we might be able to figure out how to ruin their complicated financial scheme defrauding people from coast to coast for million and millions of dollars.

Or we could just do some more kissing.

It's a tempting idea to go back to the Bedrock building and see if he shows up for work, but I don't see him doing that considering the gross malfeasance swirling in the air. Plus, I have no intention of being anywhere near there when the fallout happens from my parents' massive theft, their disappearance, and the fake FBI raid.

No, I need to find another way to contact him and can't keep walking these streets forever hoping to accidentally bump into him.

I broaden my horizons and leave myself open to the possibility of getting in touch with anyone from last night, but even with a phone I wouldn't be able to call either Taylor or Wesley. I have no idea what their numbers are but have to hope they at least got Miles's after we parted ways.

The sun and my frustration start to feel hot when it dawns on me how to contact Taylor. Struck by the realization, I stop dead in my tracks.

It happens to be in the middle of a crosswalk, and a honking car quickly gets me moving again.

The idea comes with a heavy dose of bitterness, so much so that I wonder if I'd actually be better off lingering in oncoming traffic a little longer. No, I can't let one message get in the way of finding my parents and fixing this whole situation, even if it is thoroughly unpleasant.

My walking tour of Dallas continues all the way to a branch of the public library, this one notably named after Martin Luther King Jr. Feet killing me after all of this walking, I anxiously hobble inside and bypass the bookshelves in favor of a bank of computers along the back wall.

Seeing the computers, I grit my teeth and have to force myself to march over to them, a sense of self-loathing hitting me that's even stronger than when I first had the idea. There has to be a better way to get in touch with them, I think, but there isn't.

As I sit down at a computer and begin to type the web address, every tap of the keyboard feels like a pinprick. I can't believe I've sunken so low that I'm actually doing this, or that I'm reaching out to Taylor for help. It's barely been a few days since she tried to stab me to death, and now I'm depending on her to help based on the job she lied to get in the accounting department. At least she likes numbers.

Although Taylor seemed to be swaying in the direction of getting back together with Wesley, I am terrified to think of what she put Miles through after the police whisked me away. I hope she and Wesley didn't rob Miles blind.

The next thing I know, I'm looking at the OnlyFans page for MathSlut12, featuring a selfie profile picture Taylor took of herself in the Hochatown Airbnb bathroom with not a lot of clothing on.

I involuntarily release an agonized sigh that gets the attention of a man walking by who seems to be in his early thirties. His sly grin as he leers at me makes my skin crawl, and I turn back to what I'm doing to get this over with as quickly as possible.

The pain continues when I find out I need to pay a twenty-dollar subscription fee in order to contact her. I lean back in my chair and tilt my head as far away as possible. Overcoming this hurdle is hard, even if it is Alice's money. But I can't waste too much time or the library staff will catch wind of what I'm doing and boot me out for my pervy behavior.

Subscription fee paid, I do my best to avoid looking at the pictures, not that there's anything here I haven't seen already in person. I'll be the first to say that a girl from inner-city Dallas should do whatever she can to get herself ahead, but being a little choosier about who I share my body with seems right for me.

The message I paid twenty dollars to send is as short as it gets.

"Taylor, it's Emily. I'm at the MLK library. Come get me."

I close the browser window as quickly as possible, but not before I feel a strong urge to wash my eyeballs with bleach.

Feeling like I'm unable to take another step, I trudge back out to the library's entrance and collapse onto a bench in the shade of a tree. Although I'm dirty and feel like I didn't sleep at all, I'm strangely optimistic about this working out.

Even if Taylor calls me an Uber or something, we can then

put our heads together with Miles and find my parents before they get away with what they've done. After all, we figured out their scam in a single day. Who's to say we couldn't figure out a lot more with additional time?

That's good, because the amount that we don't know seems overwhelming. My parents could be hiding out anywhere in the world, living under any names, making finding them seemingly impossible without a strong clue about where they went and what they plan to do.

And I know they plan to do something, thanks to Dad blurting out something about Mom's plan while they thought I was dead on the floor. What could be worse than what they've already done?

It takes thirty minutes for a car to arrive that seems to be here for me. It's a Subaru Outback, black with a roof rack for kayaks or other things like that.

And when the rear window rolls down and reveals Taylor's bright and smiling face, her dark-brown ponytail swishing behind her, it becomes clear she's not driving and that this isn't her car.

Miles is driving, and Wesley is beside him in the passenger seat.

They wave me over, and despite some misgivings about what they could possibly all be doing together so early, I lurch off the bench and take the rescue like I've been stranded on a deserted island.

Taylor scoots to the other side of the back seat and makes room for me to get in. When I lock eyes with Miles, I notice he isn't nearly as upbeat as she is. It looks like he slept about as well as I did. Even the dark circles under his eyes are sexy.

He takes one look at me and purses his lips, afraid to speak until he finally spits it out.

"We have some bad news," he says.

3

I nod. To be honest, I'd be more surprised if he said he had good news.

"OK, what's the bad news?" I say, bracing myself while sliding into the back seat next to Taylor, who has traded her Cowboys jersey and jeans for a floral-print sundress running to mid-thigh.

She usually goes for a much grungier, casual look, and I can't help but wonder if she's trying to impress someone. I don't mind if Miles is having a good influence on her too as long as she keeps her hands off him and sticks to Wesley, who also appears showered and rested in his usual t-shirt and basketball shorts.

From the back seat, I can only get a vague sense of Miles shaking his head.

"Let's get somewhere where I can tell you," he sighs.

I glance at Taylor, hoping she'll blurt out whatever it is right away, but all I get from her is a barely restrained cringe at my appearance. And I don't expect Wesley to even be able to fully explain whatever they've figured out, but I hope not everything that's happened since last night has to be kept a secret from me.

"Have you all been together this entire time since I left Three Tequila Floor?" I ask, my mind going to strange places trying to imagine what the three of them pulling an all-nighter together would look like.

"Oh, ahh..." Miles says, strangely giving up on whatever he was going to say. I squint at the back of his headrest, trying to figure out what that means.

"No, we all went home," Taylor says. "But I told Miles to come get us once I got your message. By the way, thank you for becoming one of my fans."

That hollow feeling returns, and my spirit cries inside of me.

Also, what Taylor said left it ambiguous whether or not she was with Wesley last night, but I decide that's something I don't want to know more about.

Wesley twists around to look back at me, a self-indulgent grin on his big face.

"We didn't leave the bar right away though. After the cops dragged you out of there kicking and screaming, a lot of people wanted to know what you'd done," he says.

"I wasn't kicking and screaming!" I say.

Groaning, I look out the window as we cruise through traffic. Wherever we're going, I hope we get there soon.

"That's only the beginning of what he said," Taylor adds under her breath, and I jerk my head back at Wesley in time to see him shrugging and facing forward.

"Oh, come on. You wouldn't want us to miss capitalizing on that fun," he says as if it's blatantly obvious. "So I may have told some people you're a serial killer. Now you're a legend."

I barely have time to flinch before I'm shouting back at him.

"I'm not a serial killer!" I say. That should be self-evident for most people, but it occurs to me that I should elaborate. "Being a serial killer means you've killed more than one person."

Although I'm talking to Wesley, I'm looking at the back of

Miles's head. I can't see his face, even in the rearview mirror, and I don't want him to judge me negatively.

Everyone has a dark past. Mine just happens to be from a few days ago.

"There's still time for you to get there," Wesley says.

Now he's grating on my nerves, and I grit my teeth.

"Are you forgetting the exact same could be said about you?" I ask.

Bringing up his encounter in the dark woods of Hochatown with an actual serial killer manages to shut him up, and I hope he remembers how reticent and disturbed he was when he was telling me what he had to do to stop the one-eyed creep from finding his way back to my unconscious body on the beach.

"I don't think any of us were thinking clearly," Taylor says, seemingly to herself.

I watch her out of the corner of my eye, and I can't tell if she's actually regretful of if it's an act. She had a big hand in Alice's death too, but determining what caused it and who's really to blame is like riding a merry-go-round.

Ultimately, my parents sent her to take me out during a weekend trip together. After everything I talked to my mom and dad about in the executive office, it occurs to me that I have some bad news of my own to share with the three of them.

Miles pulls into a ground-floor parking garage in a relatively nice neighborhood full of multi-story apartment buildings. The realization that we're here distracts me from the uncomfortable memories of Alice and what this is all about, and I gawk at a part of town that's at once modest and decent yet vastly nicer than where I live or have ever lived.

I mean, there's hardly any garbage on the streets here. There are trees around. And I'd probably have to search for a good long time to find any homeless people.

Miles pulls into a parking spot and shuts off the engine.

"I'm on the fifth floor," he says, and a look of shock crosses Taylor's face too.

Even though he's barely arrived in Dallas and has only been working for one day, Miles already has a lifestyle that is a cut above all of the rest of us. I even see Wesley giving him another appraisal, which makes my heart lurch when I recognize the way he checks out potential scam targets.

From the parking garage to the hallways to the elevator, everything is reasonably nice though definitely not brand new. When we get to his floor, Miles welcomes us into a three-room apartment with a nice couch, an actual table and chairs, and a bed that has a frame, not merely a mattress on the floor.

So much of what I see are such simple, basic things that I've somehow more or less never been able to have. This place has to cost at least a couple of thousand dollars a month, and it smells nice too. On top of that, Miles is relatively neat, scarcely a shirt and a few socks on the floor that he quickly scoops up and tosses away.

Not only would it disappoint him horribly if he knew every bad thing I've done in my life, but he'd think I'm a slob as well. I stand awkwardly in the middle of the room, noticing all of the stuff he has everywhere. He has his own laptop, some board games, and books. So many books.

"Nice place," I say, trying not to act too impressed. "Was it tough to find?"

In a way, I'm hoping to distract Miles from noticing Taylor and Wesley snooping in his kitchenette and closet space. He glances in the direction of his bedroom, where the bed is nicely made. When I picture myself on it, my cheeks burn.

"No, it wasn't hard at all," he says simply, shrugging to drive home the point that decently nice things are readily available to anyone with enough money for them.

Taylor has flopped on the brown suede couch, and I drift

toward Wesley, who is perusing the countertop, the only cluttered space in the apartment. There's mail, some paperwork and swag from Bedrock, some stones he may be collecting, and a thin little iPod that catches our attention.

I grin, remembering when those were commonly used, not that I ever had one. Wesley picks it up to give it a closer look. It's the kind of small thing that could easily get lost or misplaced, and Wesley taps a button, seeing that it works.

In a flash, I realize where this is going, and right as Wesley twists to the side and brings his hand around to his pocket, I smack his wrist and knock the device back onto the counter, right as Miles turns to glance in our direction.

Embarrassed, I smile innocently, even as Wesley gives me an annoyed look. I lean forward, elbows on the counter, to block him from touching the iPod again.

"I think I'm as ready for your bad news as I'm going to be," I say to Miles, hoping to get this show on the road before Taylor or Wesley cause more trouble.

Miles has a recliner next to the couch, and he takes a seat on the armrest, exchanging a look with Taylor before scratching his messy hair and directing his attention to me.

"After you were taken away, we were able to examine the company accounts, thanks to Taylor's access to the accounting department's system—"

"My pleasure," Taylor says quickly, taking credit and lifting her chin.

"Yeah," Miles continues, put off by the interruption, "and there was a major withdrawal from the company's accounts. Probably ninety-nine percent of what was there is gone. We're talking hundreds of millions of dollars. And that's not even the worst part. All of the records about the transaction have been wiped from the system."

I nod feverishly, trying to act surprised.

"That's terrible," I say, and Miles shakes his head in dismay, probably thinking of the millions of people who have had their retirements and life savings wiped out in one fell swoop.

"It's unbelievable to think that based on solely what's left, Bedrock is basically flat broke now. It won't even be able to make payroll in a week. Someone had to have very high-level access to be able to pull this off."

"You're right."

"And here's what's crazy too. The FBI was just at the office checking for this very thing, but somehow it still went through. It seems impossible. Who would do something like this?" he asks, gazing at the ceiling as if he's looking for some divine intervention to provide an answer.

But Miles doesn't need to look up, because I know the part he's missing. I pull away from the counter, giving Wesley a stern glance not to steal anything while I'm busy talking, and come around close to the other side of the couch.

"I know exactly who would do this," I say regretfully, wishing this wasn't the truth of it.

Miles's eyes widen. "Who? Terry Glint? Candace Roberts?"

I inhale through my teeth, bracing myself.

"Yes and no. Those are fake names for people who never existed. These fake identities and really this entire company were created for the sole purpose of executing this Ponzi scheme. The people doing this are my parents."

I don't know what kind of a reaction I was expecting, but it's not a blank stare. Taylor at least cringes, while Wesley watches me intently. Miles's mouth slowly drifts open, and eventually something comes out of it.

"Your parents? Like your mom and dad?"

"Duh, that's what 'parents' means," Wesley speaks up, snickering.

"Not always," Taylor says, crossing her arms over her chest.

I raise a hand, trying to calm everyone down.

"I wish it weren't true, but I promise I'm not lying. The FBI agents who took me from the police aren't real FBI agents. They work for my parents and were part of a ruse to disrupt the office while they stole all of that money. The thugs brought me up to the executive suite, and I saw my parents with my own eyes. They're making their getaway now," I explain, my urgency coming through.

It goes without saying that they need to be stopped.

Taylor lowers her eyes at me.

"Most people who promise they're not lying are lying," she says, and I jerk my head in her direction. "Do you really expect us to believe you caught your parents embezzling hundreds of millions of dollars and they let you watch and walk out of there?"

I scowl at her, getting really tired of how she never believes me when I'm telling the truth.

"As a matter of fact, they tried to shoot me and then rushed out when they thought I was dead. They're going somewhere far away, somewhere with a beach."

Miles gets up from the chair, standing straight with clenched fists.

"They can't get away with this. Trying to kill people, absconding with huge sums of money? There's no way we can let this go," he says.

I find myself grinning along with him. This is exactly what I want, and my desire to get back at them burns in my chest.

Taylor leans forward, gripping the front of the couch.

"OK, so where are they going?" she asks me.

I look at her with full knowledge that I can't be mad at her about this question, yet I'm incensed all the same.

"I don't know. All they said was that there'd be a beach," I confess.

"That only narrows it down to pretty much every country in the world," Wesley scoffs. "For all we know, they're going to Hochatown."

I hope not.

Wincing, I lay the rest of it on them.

"That's not all. You don't understand what my parents are like. Not only could they be anywhere in the world, but they could have any name you could imagine, maybe even several of them. There's no telling what they could be doing or where they could end up."

The moan that escapes from Miles scalds my ears, and I watch him hang his head.

"So it's hopeless. They've disappeared, there's no way to track them, and they're going to get away with everything," he says, crestfallen.

It's only a few steps for me to set my hand on his shoulder, encouraging him to look up at me. He's not as experienced with rip-offs and scammers as I am, and I need to take charge and show him that we can make something even out of nothing.

"Don't give up so easily. There's still a way we might be able to find out what they're up to before it's too late," I say with an emboldened look, my hand still resting on his shoulder. I can feel his warmth.

"How? What is it?" he asks, some life coming back into his eyes.

"My sister might know," I say.

"You mean the dead one?" Taylor snorts, causing me to turn around. It's comforting having Miles by my side.

"Yes," I say without explanation.

They all give me a wary look.

"So we're going to visit her in a graveyard?" Wesley asks, rolling his eyes for Taylor.

I take a moment to look at the two of them, each with dozens of crimes between them, not to mention an active murder investigation ongoing, assaults, thefts, and surely much more that I don't even know about.

The smirk comes easily.

"No, we're going to prison."

4
_____

Warm water drizzles down my face and drips from my chin, joining the water pooling around my feet, brownish from all of the dirt and grime I've been covered in. I'm hopeful that it all makes it down the drain and doesn't leave Miles's shower as filthy as I was.

A flurry of scrubbing and washing ensues, though Miles is conspicuously short on shower supplies. I had to hunt to find even a single tiny washcloth, which I practically destroy with how vigorously I drag it against every inch of my sandpaper-like skin.

And then there's his selection of personal hygiene products. Actually, "selection" isn't an appropriate way to describe it, since there's really only one bottle that I have no choice but to use liberally. I guess I won't have to worry about dandruff for a while.

Being clean is a step in the right direction, and I top it off by borrowing—not stealing—some of Miles's clothes, a plaid flannel shirt that has no business being in toasty Texas and a pair of jeans that other than being tight in the thighs and hips will suffice in a pinch. The clothes I had been wearing should probably be burned or disposed of in a toxic waste dump.

When I walk out of the bathroom, my hair still damp and some steam escaping alongside me, I find Miles at his computer working on something. Taylor and Wesley made themselves scarce as soon as the prospect of visiting a prison came up, leaving the two of us in his apartment.

Miles glances up in my direction from the computer screen and then freezes, struck by something and staring with his big brown eyes and light-pink lips, making him seem slightly in a trance. For a second I worry I've left the fly open. Who knows how these men's clothes work? But then I realize he's looking at me.

"You clean up nice," he says.

I play it cool. "Are you saying I didn't look good when I was a walking dustbin?"

He chuckles, and I take it as a double win.

The warmth and comfort of being fresh out of the shower makes me feel better but doesn't give me a ton more energy, and I tip onto the couch, which is as soft as a cloud. Sitting up straight, I try to focus my sluggish mind on the task at hand.

Miles swivels in his chair to face me, and I can see him grinning slightly at me wearing his clothes. Maybe I should've left a couple of buttons undone.

"Are you sure you want to see your sister right away?" he asks, which sounds like a crazy question.

"I haven't seen her in ten years. I'd crawl all the way there through broken glass if I had to," I say, hands tucked in my lap. I need to go so badly, but at the same time I feel like I couldn't even get off this couch if I wanted to.

He purses his lips and scratches his cheek.

"And where is the 'there' we need to get to exactly?"

I look away and sigh.

"I don't know that."

I try to avoid his skeptical look.

"Is she in a federal or state prison? Maximum security? Is she even in Texas? You say this was a while ago, so was it a juvenile detention center? If so, how do we know she's even in there anymore? Are you sure your parents weren't lying to you?"

The questions bombard me, each one feeling like a knock on the head. I raise a hand before I start to crack under the pressure. My sister is out there somewhere, and she needs me right now. Truth be told, I need her too, or I'll never find my thieving parents.

"No, I believe them that she's in prison. Give me one second to close my eyes and try to remember if my mom gave away any other clues."

When I open my eyes, the computer chair is vacant, and Miles is at the kitchen counter eating a sandwich. The light is coming in through the window differently, though I'm still sitting upright on the couch. My head still swims but isn't as crushing as before. I clear my dry throat and swallow, blinking rapidly to shake off the fogginess.

"What are you doing?" I ask, now noticing that his computer isn't on anymore.

He looks at me for a moment.

"I'm having lunch."

I snicker, appreciating how rare it is for him to make a faux pas.

"Do you mean breakfast? It's like 8 a.m."

Miles covers his mouth to hide a grin and shakes his head.

"Not anymore. You slept for four hours."

My eyes widen, and then I glare at the couch as if it were at fault for this. "Really? I don't have time to waste sleeping," I say when another thought strikes me. "And what were you doing this whole time when I was out cold while sitting up on your couch?"

Miles takes another bite of his sandwich, disconcertingly calm considering how frantic I am about the lost time.

"I did some research and made a few calls. Your sister is serving a sentence in Linda Woodman State Jail, a women's prison in Gatesville."

That gets my excitement up and my heart beating faster. This is way more helpful than what I'd imagine a guy would do while I was unconscious for hours on his couch, leering at me if nothing else. I've built up so much suspicion and cynicism and self-defense mechanisms, but it crosses my mind that maybe with Miles I don't need them.

He's done all the work for me, and I got to sleep. Is this what can happen in a real relationship not based on exploiting each other or anyone around for as much as a person can get?

"That's amazing," I say, already getting to my feet. "How far away is Gatesville? What about visiting hours?"

With a new sense of purpose and overflowing enthusiasm, I'd start walking if I had to. Miles raises a hand.

"We've got plenty of time. Here, get something to eat first. Gatesville is about two hours away. Visiting hours run all afternoon."

I can't argue with that, but I'm still anxious to get going and want to get out the door before I've even finished the sandwich Miles made for me. Ham isn't my favorite, but choking something down is one of the few things standing between me and my sister, finding out how she ended up where she is, and having her tell me how to hunt down our parents.

Once I've eaten enough to survive a two-hour drive, we leave his apartment behind to make the journey to the women's prison. After not seeing my sister for ten years, I feel like I'll die if I don't go right away. Or maybe it's that a part of me died when my parents told me she was killed in a car accident. Now I can come fully back to life again with Melanie back in it.

We do have to make a quick stop near my apartment to quickly snatch some of my personal effects now that I'm no longer trying to pass as Alice. I don't let Miles come in with me. In fact, I have him park around the corner and hoof the last leg alone.

But after that we're hitting the road to Gatesville, and this time I'm in the passenger seat. It's nice up here and also much more pleasant without Taylor or Wesley interjecting their antics into serious conversations all the time.

We start out on Route 35S through the arid Texas country-side. There's not much for me to see, and I end up sneaking glances at the most appealing view around. Miles is focused on the road, his profile fixed in place to my left. He drives with one hand on the wheel, his other resting on his thigh.

I take a deep breath, feeling Miles's flannel shirt squeeze my chest area a little, not exactly cut to my shape. Good thing the air conditioner is going, or else I'd have the garment soaked through with sweat.

"Aren't you glad you didn't have to go back to Bedrock today?" I ask in a joking tone, trying to keep things light.

But Miles either doesn't notice my grin or refuses to share in it. He scratches his neck and grimaces. It's that thoughtful look he got while trying to work through the Q Fund fraud, but this time it's more foreboding and discontented. Something on his mind is making him unhappy.

Is it possible he's not exactly thrilled to be spending most of his day ferrying me to a women's prison way outside of town?

He sighs audibly, and I start to feel nervous about whatever he's going to come out with next. After rubbing his forehead, he glances at me, and it's not the warm and fuzzy kind.

"I hate to say this, but I'm having a hard time with some of this stuff," he says, my nerves ratcheting up. "After you were taken away, that time I spent with Wesley and Taylor, I've never met anybody like them in my life."

As glad as I am that he doesn't lump me in with them, it's not as much of a relief as it should be. There's no point deluding myself that I don't have things in common with them and haven't made many of the same mistakes.

"You want to vent about the two of them? Don't get me started," I say, still trying to have some levity about it, but he merely shakes his head. I can see the disgust on his face.

"They are not normal. Wesley is the kind of guy who'd try to lie to me about my own name, and Taylor strikes me as barely holding on. She acts normal enough, but I feel like she could be set off in a snap and go completely crazy."

I swallow, not able to find much amusement in any of that. Sighing, I glance out the window, trying not to take it personally. At least he didn't see Wesley trying to steal the iPod right off his kitchen counter.

"There wasn't a good chance to tell you about them. Wesley keeps saying he wants to change, that some of the things that happened at the lake were too intense for him, but I don't know if he'll ever be able to. And as for Taylor, she doesn't have a good background or a good family either. She's trying to hold it all together, like I am," I say.

That gets me another look from him, his brown eyes washing over me. I keep waiting for a harsh judgment to break into them, condescension, dismissiveness, but instead I feel like he's seeing me for who I am now, not for who I was.

"You're stronger than they'll ever be," he says, though I have to strain to hear it even with the stereo off.

It's nice to hear, but only time will tell if I'm strong enough for what I'll have to do to make things right and get through this. Even right now I feel like I'm breaking in two at the prospect of seeing my sister, the person I still love most in the world but who is basically a total stranger.

Seeing hints of the tall cement walls of Linda Woodman State Jail appear on the horizon saps all the energy I have, making me wonder if I'll even have the strength to go through with filling the hole in my life I've lived with for ten years.

5

I've slept, eaten, and washed, but when I stare up at the imposing, austere walls of the women's prison with the barbed wire fencing and lookout towers, I realize what I really need is a drink.

It's almost enough to make me want to endure another girls' night like last night, but the chill I get simply looking at the prison facade freezes me in place.

"Are you OK?" Miles asks, stretching his legs next to his car while I'm standing here in the parking lot in the sweltering heat.

My startled look in his direction betrays my reluctance. Usually I'm not such a wimp, especially after five years of living on the streets. Everyone acted tough as nails, but deep down this is the very thing everyone was afraid of.

We were afraid of getting caught, being held accountable, losing our freedom, losing our lives. But this is my sister's life and has been for the past five years.

I still haven't looked up any articles relating to the trial or sentencing, which I know are out there. A part of me still doesn't want to know the truth. The lies that my sister was dead and that my parents had been thrown in jail were not comforting, but finding out what really happened that made things like this seems worse.

"Yes, of course. I'm always OK. I'll let you know when I'm done," I say.

He squints at me, some sweat forming on his brow. This flannel shirt already feels like I'm wearing a furnace.

"What? I'm going in," he says, and I look at him strangely.

"But it's a prison," I say.

"So what?"

My eyes widen, and for a moment I'm speechless. He's not at all afraid, and not simply because this is a women's prison he couldn't ever actually end up in. He has a clean conscience and has nothing to fear. As for myself, a deep sense of dread sets in that I could easily end up in my sister's shoes very soon.

"Keep up," I say, setting off quickly in the hopes that by taking charge I can bury my trepidation.

There are a few others vehicles around, other visitors coming in and out, but mostly this is simply a fortress in the middle of the desert where the sun beats down and not much can grow.

Even the front doors are difficult to open, as if they're warning me not to come in, but they're only the beginning of the challenges I encounter to actually get inside. There are corrections officers who check my ID and take my fingerprints, something I do despite my jaw quivering.

Maybe I'm already signing over my life by coming here, but for my sister I have to do it. Still, there's no warrant for my arrest out there. It's doubtful this Texas state prison has any connection to an Oklahoma county sheriff running a murder investigation that I'm deeply involved in.

Miles actually cheerfully says hi like he's walking into a bookstore to browse. The corrections officer, a middle-aged woman in a too-small uniform, merely gives him a look before turning back to me.

"Who are you here for?" she asks.

I swallow. "Melanie Marks."

She narrows her eyes at me. "No really, who? She never gets visitors."

I have to take a deep breath to calm myself. It seems like anything can set me off in this dark, uncomfortable space.

"You saw my ID and know we have the same last name. The only reason I've never come is that I didn't know my sister was here."

The officer scoffs, "You didn't know your own sister was here? Some sister you are."

Triggered, I clench my fists and open my mouth to rain fire down upon her, but Miles puts his hand on my shoulder before I can commence an epic rant about how I'm not a bad sister and none of this is my fault.

A smirk from the officer signals that she thinks she's won, but Miles is right. She doesn't matter, and she doesn't need the whole story about why I've only come to visit Melanie now. What does matter is getting to my sister as fast as possible, and keeping my mouth shut accomplishes that.

A few minutes later, we're cleared to enter a large room divided in the middle by a series of booths, plexiglass dividing the two sides and a phone on each side for the visitor and incarcerated to communicate. Puke-green linoleum floor, wobbly ceiling fans, and a few visitors and corrections officers complete the picture.

Miles's closed-lip smile and nod seem weighty, and I'm glad he's come here with me, even if only to the edge of the room by the door, where he takes one of the chairs against the back wall. He's the only one sitting there.

"You can do this," he says, and my nerves are so brittle that

I'm tempted to snap at him too. Of course I can do this. Does he think I have any trouble talking to my own sister?

"Thank you," I mutter, turning quickly before I say something that makes this worse.

I walk to the booth straight across from Miles, unable to pretend my nerves don't exist any longer. Maybe I can't do this. What if she's not the person I remember? What if I put my foot in my mouth and say something stupid that she'll never forgive?

In some ways, perhaps having her dead was easier. Then she'd always be this image of perfection in my memory instead of a living and breathing person with her own opinions and beliefs that might conflict with mine.

A loud buzz snaps me out of my gushing thoughts, and one of the corrections officers on the other side pulls open a thick steel door. I find myself holding my breath, knowing what's coming yet not knowing.

A woman in an orange jumpsuit steps through, and I recognize her immediately, Melanie. She's not shackled or anything but has a muted expression, hair brushing her shoulders, and weariness around her eyes that makes her seem older than someone barely old enough to purchase alcohol.

My sister is alive.

My jaw is quivering again, and I struggle to hold it together. I want to leap out of my seat, break through the glass, hold her tight, and bawl my eyes out that she didn't die in a car accident like my parents told me.

All I can do to try to keep my composure is to keep surveying her, and it doesn't take me long to make some notable observations. After she takes only a few steps, I'm taken aback at her size. She's not any taller than me, and a lot is hidden under the orange jumpsuit, but I quickly get the sense that whatever prison workout routine she's doing has made her a beast.

It's like she's a dark-haired version of me who looks like she can pick up a car. Maybe that's an exaggeration, but I wouldn't bet against her even if she took on a gym monkey like Wesley. And I get more of a sense of her eyes. It's not so much weariness as it is hardened watchfulness and confidence.

My sister is stronger than I am.

When she spots me, I rise out of my seat and stand there blankly in awe of what I'm seeing and that it's her. I don't pretend for a second that it's good she's in there regardless of how she looks or acts, but I know it hasn't broken her.

There's no time for me to think about how to act or what to do. I'm barely conscious of anything but her and may be waving or smiling or crying, but I can't be sure. It's Melanie, my sister.

She comes over to the window, largely expressionless until she chews her cheek a little, and I'm not sure what that means. Maybe she's used to guarding her feelings or has to be careful of how she acts because of what other inmates might hear, but I don't mind being the big sister and taking charge. It's a role I've missed.

"I can't believe it's you!" I say, tearing up and bringing a hand to my mouth while the other reaches out and touches the glass between us. This thin, clear plane seems like such a big barrier.

Pursing her lips, Melanie points to her ear, and I understand that she can't hear anything I'm saying.

We sit down, and I'm able to get a better look at her even though there are quite a few smudges on the glass. She's more tanned than I am, apparently getting out into the hot sun some. But besides that, the rosy cheeks are as I remember them, the cute chin. Her eyes have the same kind of detached haze to them that she'd get after watching TV for way too long.

Phones to our ears, I can't help gushing again. "Thank you so much for meeting with me. I don't even know where to start. I'm sorry, I guess. They said no one comes to visit you."

She nods absently.

"Hi, Emily," she says, not exactly the warm welcome I would've expected, no putting our hands to the glass together, but it's not completely emotionless.

"Do you know how long it's been? Ten years," I say, shaking my head. "How have you been?"

She bites her lip like it's a hard question and is unsure of how to respond.

"I'm fine and dandy," she says then leans to the side and looks over my shoulder. I don't have to guess to know who she's checking out. "But it looks like you've been doing very well for yourself. I'm glad one of us is getting some action."

I blink, having some mental whiplash hearing my little sister talk about "getting action." She's not twelve anymore and has interests beyond ponies and working in an ice cream shop so she can get free ice cream.

I'm glad to see Melanie breaking out of her daze, but I don't want her to get the wrong idea about Miles or think that I've brought him to show off or something.

"Oh, it's not really like that," I say quickly.

"Come on, no reason to hold back. How is he?" she asks with a grin. I have to take a deep breath, fully aware of the part of him she's asking about.

I swallow, the phone pressed tight to my ear.

"I wouldn't know. We haven't...anything really."

She narrows her eyes at me, and then her line of sight drifts down. This conversation is already way off track with no signs of veering in the right direction.

"Wait a second, are you wearing his clothes?" she gasps.

I unconsciously glance down, as if I need to check if I still have on the clothes I'd worn all day. A burning feeling grows in my chest, and I'm in disbelief that she caught me.

"They are, but it's a long story. I only met him yesterday, and he—"

"Emily Marks!" she says, lighting up. "You've become such a minx."

"No, you don't understand!"

She lowers her eyes at me, not buying any of it.

"Did you sleep at his place?" she asks.

My breath catches. Oh no, this is not going to help my case.

"Well, yes, but it wasn't at night."

Her grin widens into a self-indulgent smile that I'm happy to see, though I wish it weren't due to her thinking I'm some kind of prowling seductress. I can only imagine that around here there's a dearth of entertainment and that a little provocative gossip can go a long way, but I came here to talk about our parents, not Miles.

"So let me get this straight," Melanie begins, shaking her head and making her hair sway around the phone. "You met a cute guy yesterday, you slept at his place, you're in his clothes, he came with you to a hole like this to see me, and nothing is going on?"

Her raised eyebrow and sneaky smirk are begging me to disagree with her.

I sigh.

"Not yet, at least. If you have to know, we kissed once, but that's it. You know, these things take time," I say, trying not to get frustrated.

In my teens, I'd imagine all the nights we could've spent gossiping about boys, but none of them involved armed guards, orange jumpsuits, or plexiglass dividers.

"I know all about things taking time," she says grimly, and my insides curdle. Maybe I should've spun some yarns about a scorching twenty-four-hour romance just to make her happy and distract her from her life in here, but I've been trying to lie less and imagine that in the long run it would only make her resent where she is more.

"Anyway, I didn't come here to show him to you. There's something I need to talk to you about."

Before I can say more, I catch Melanie looking me dead in the eyes. She nods slowly and leans closer to the glass.

"Yes, of course. You came to tell me that you stopped them. That's such a relief," she says, running her hand through her loose black strands, more resembling Dad's than Mom's.

I gaze at her.

"Wait, what?"

Her look sours into something quizzical, and now she's regarding me skeptically.

"You found out what Mom and Dad were up to with their Bedrock company and put an end to it," she says, nodding emphatically to drive home her confidence.

My mouth agape, I can hardly think of what to say. I'd only figured out what they were doing yesterday, but somehow my sister already knew about it all the way out here in prison in the middle of the desert.

"How... So you know they were the ones running Bedrock?" I say, awestruck.

Melanie glares at me, as if the answer is as clear as the glass between us.

"Of course I know. How do you think you found out about the job there in the first place?"

6

Melanie sits and waits patiently, calm and placid as though she's got all the time in the world, while I'm having another mental implosion.

She isn't really suggesting that she had a hand in all of this, is she?

I start and then stop, shaking my head before I can finally spit something out. "What do you mean, I found out about the job at Bedrock because of you?"

She leans farther forward on the narrow surface on her side of the glass, holding her head in one propped hand with the phone to her opposite ear.

"It's just what it sounds like."

With that helpful comment, I get annoyed that I'm constantly behind and racing to catch up. Wouldn't I have known if my sister did something to get me my financial planner job? This is ridiculous.

"You must be mistaken. I found out about the Bedrock position thanks to a flyer in my mailbox. They probably gave them to everybody in the building, if not everybody in hundreds of buildings around Dallas," I say.

I vividly remember opening my mailbox one day and seeing the glossy flyer featuring the Bedrock logo and a picture of a successful young woman in a business suit. I was wearing dirty sweatpants and a torn t-shirt. The resentment bubbled up immediately, and rather than throw it away like all the rest of the junk mail I got, I decided to cook up my fake résumé. That was almost a month ago now, and as they say, the rest is history.

My sister shakes her head in a way that seems somewhat condescending.

"No, Emily. There was only one copy of that flyer made, and it was only put in one mailbox, yours."

"But how could—"

"I have friends outside of these walls," she explains before I can even utter my obvious question.

That leaves me sitting back, arms crossed, trying to think it all through. It doesn't nearly add up with everything else I know. My eyebrows scrunch up, and I feel my eyes watering despite my attempts to keep calm.

I feel the pain before I can even understand why it's hitting me.

"But that means... You knew where I lived. You knew I was there. You could've contacted me. Somebody, your friend, could've told me where you were and what was happening to you. Why did you keep me in the dark?" I ask, nearly breathless.

Melanie isn't so blasé now, instead sitting up and mirroring my emotion. Something I said hit home with her, possibly because she'd spent time pondering the same things herself.

"Emily, please don't put that on me right now. I can't handle it. What good would it have done if I'd let you know where I was only for you not to be able to do anything about it? I spared you from five years of the guilt and agony I've felt, which would've been completely pointless to share with you!"

I'm shaking my head, my heart telling me I would've rather

known the truth but my gut saying she may well be right. I would've tortured myself knowing she was locked away in prison. My horrible living situation for the past five years couldn't seem any worse, but with that in my head I would've been despondent as well.

"But how did you even know where I was or what I was doing? Mom and Dad told me you died—"

"In a car accident," Melanie cuts in, growing somber while I nod forcefully. "That's what they told me too, and they even put on a little fake funeral with a few random drunks they probably paid to show up. Then once I was in here with nothing to do but think about everything they lied about, I realized they must've been lying about your death too."

My eyes widen into giant saucers. It's too much to take, and not just how they gave her the same phony spiel about a car accident that they peddled to me.

My sister is smarter than I am.

"You figured it out," I say, full-on crying now and barely able to hold the phone. "And I was too self-absorbed or deluded to realize it was all a lie and you were still out there. I can't believe how stupid I am to believe anything they ever said."

I put my head down, unable to look at my sister and her orange jumpsuit any longer. The shame is overwhelming, knowing that any day for the past ten years I could've realized the truth but didn't. I blindly accepted Mom and Dad's lies, never questioning them, even though I had every reason in the world to.

"Hey, Emily... Emily?" Melanie finally has to resort to knocking on the glass to get me to look up. Her eyes are scrunched up, but she's holding it together much better than I am, probably because she has far less to be embarrassed about.

My mind feels numb, but there's still so much I don't know.

"How did you end up in here? I thought it was Mom and Dad going to prison in their fraud case."

Melanie purses her lips and flinches away, another sore subject. She gazes blankly at the corner of the divider, no doubt reliving horrors I couldn't imagine.

"The fraud trial," she says, smacking her lips like the words have a nasty taste to them. "I'd barely had contact with Mom and Dad after your accident. They told me they couldn't bear to have me around anymore, since I reminded them of you. They sent me off to Dad's brother's house in Plano, Uncle Tommy.

"It was strange to live there. He had no wife, no kids, not much empathy of any kind. It was almost like living in a hotel, except it was a relative's house. Years passed, and then I started volunteering at a nursing home, putting on activities for the old people and helping out a little here and there. That was when Mom and Dad showed up.

"I was surprised to see them and even more shocked when they said they wanted to help. Except they hardly helped at all and mostly liked hanging around and talking to people in the lounge. I didn't realize what they were doing, giving people hard luck stories and trying to rob the residents, change their wills, get involved in their family affairs, and so on.

"One day they stopped showing up, and it took a while for me to find out it was because they were arrested for running this fraud scheme on the residents. Occasionally I would hear tidbits about whatever was going on. Uncle Tommy grew talkative for the first time and caught wind of some things."

Melanie tenses up, shuddering, and a dark pit grows in my stomach, dreading what's going to come next. I can see the writing on the wall clearly enough. This is the part that ruined my sister's life forever. It takes a snarl and some gritted teeth for my sister to get up the gumption to keep going.

"Then the detectives came for me. Mom and Dad claimed

that I was the ringleader of the whole scheme and that I forced them to do it, guilting them into it because of their love for me, and they agreed to testify against me for a lighter sentence—I think they ended up with nothing more than some community service and probation.

"I was flat broke and couldn't afford a high-powered lawyer. My public defender was a complete pushover. The judge didn't see the truth and couldn't care less. The victims just wanted anybody to be held accountable. There were cheers in the courtroom when I was convicted of the fraud charges, Mom and Dad louder than any others as they celebrated from the spectator seating. And now I'm here."

I don't know what to say after all of that. My parents' behavior has been too horrendous to shock me anymore, and nothing could accurately describe how wretched they had been to us.

"I'm so sorry," I say at last, feeling like some sympathy is the best I can do.

Melanie shakes her head, uncomfortable but tolerating it.

"They made me their escape goat," she says, shaking her head and sounding her age for the first time.

"I think you mean scapegoat."

She rolls her eyes at me.

"That's what I said. They just got on my back and rode me out of trouble while I could only baa and mewl as I got sucked into it."

I nod, going along with it but trying to think of how to get her back on track.

"Can I ask one thing though? Surely there must have been previous job openings or something at Bedrock. If you knew they were up to something, why didn't you alert me earlier?"

Melanie sighs and switches the phone to her other ear.

"If you got to them too early, they would be able to wriggle out of their scheme or pretend nothing was wrong. I don't know what they're doing but assume it has to be bad. Then I heard that a few months ago Congress passed a law requiring more reporting from business owners, and I knew that would trigger them to do whatever they were planning. That's why it's so good you stopped them when you did."

A sly smile crosses her face, perhaps something rare she's able to take real satisfaction in while in prison. My sister's own sneaky plan to get back at my parents was an impressively good one, but there's one obvious problem, and there's no way to avoid bringing it up now.

"Yeah, about that..." I say, hemming and hawing. "I didn't exactly come here to tell you that I stopped them from stealing all the money they hoarded from their Ponzi scheme. It's more that they got away and I need your help figuring out where they went."

A blank look freezes onto Melanie's face until it cracks all at once. She leaps up and smacks the plexiglass, phone dropping, and I can only assume it would be my head if this divider wasn't here.

"Emily, no! What? No!" she howls loudly enough for me to still make it out.

A corrections officer suddenly appears, shouting at her and grabbing her by the shoulder. Emily immediately puts her hands up and relents. Eventually the officer lets her sit back down and pick up the phone again.

"But they can't be gone," she says, anguish in her voice that wasn't there before. I swallow, my discomfort growing.

"I do want to stop them, but I haven't yet. I only found them at the last minute. They were literally on their way out the door, and Mom tried to shoot me before she left. If they didn't think I was dead, I actually would be and wouldn't be here right now!" I argue, pleading with her. "All I need is for you to tell me where they might be."

Gritted teeth and face contorted, Melanie looks like she's in agony.

"They're at the Bedrock building! That's why I sent you there!"

I'm clutching the phone way harder than I need to.

"I'm sorry, Melanie. I did my best, but I'm not done yet. Do you have any idea where I might find them? It sounds like they went somewhere with a beach. That's all I know."

She couldn't meet my eyes anymore, instead glaring off to the side, lips pursed and scowling hotly.

"This was my chance to get back at them and find a way out of here. I thought if they were actually busted, someone would figure out that my sentence is all wrong. Then I could go free. I believed in you, Emily. I still do, but I don't know how it gets fixed now."

My disappointment in myself is bone deep, and knowing I've blown what should've been an easy chance doesn't provide any comfort. But she doesn't know what I've been through or how I only figured out what was going on when it was already too late. I shake my head, grasping for a way to salvage this situation.

"I'm not going to stop until I find them and get you out of here. I promise you that. Do you hear me? Even if it's the last thing I do. Every single night before I fall asleep, I have waking nightmares about what happened and what I've had to do, but then I dream about movies and popcorn and doing other silly, simple things with you that we should've had all along. I promise we're going to have our girls' time," I say even as my voice goes hoarse.

Gazing at me through lowered eyes, Melanie is wary and nods reluctantly, likely because she has no other choice. She's barely hanging on to hope and knows this is her only chance. If

Mom and Dad are gone for good, so are her chances of getting out.

"All I have is girls' time."

The corrections officer comes back, taking her out of the chair and telling her that her visiting time is up. I'm left there holding the phone to my ear as they prod her back to the door.

She takes one last look over her shoulder at me, her black hair swaying lightly above that big orange jumpsuit, her eyes with a beaten but desperate look, before she's swallowed back up in the belly of the women's prison.

7

The ride back to Dallas is uneventful and quiet, with Miles getting acquainted with a new side of me that he's never seen before.

Moody, irritated Emily doesn't want the music on. She doesn't want to talk about what happened. And the last thing she wants to do is joke around, have fun, or plan something enjoyable for the rest of the evening once we're back at his place.

All she wants to do is stew in her staggering disappointment that things could've gone so rotten.

I can't avoid blaming myself, even though I had zero inklings that there was a chance I could've stopped my parents and saved my sister all in one fell swoop last night. But that possibility, never within reach and only visible in hindsight, haunts me more than I could have imagined.

Miles does his best to accommodate me while I'm busy ruining our first night together. Yes, I have no intention of going anywhere else, especially to my apartment, which is a dump I'm about to get evicted from anyway. He gets the hint quickly enough and gives me some space to sulk and be alone, eventually doing some things on his computer I have no interest in.

Then, while I'm huddled on the recliner, I see him get a blanket out of a closet, settle on the couch, and pull it over him.

"What are you doing?" I ask, snapping at him.

"I'm getting some sleep."

"But your bed is in there." I point, in case it's not clear to him where I'm talking about in his apartment.

"Goodnight, Emily."

I open my mouth to argue, but he's shutting his eyes and closing off my opportunity for debate. That leaves me to take a long look in the direction of the bedroom before sighing in disgust.

Now I have a new thing to be frustrated about, having to be irritated when he's being so nice to me. I'm lying on his soft bed, alone with my arms crossed tight over my middle and my knees touching while I'm staring at the ceiling. Even breathing seems difficult with this level of dissatisfaction eroding my mental state.

Getting past how I'm not doing any of the things I'd imagined myself doing on this bed, I again return to the conundrum of my parents, how they could be anywhere in the world under any name imaginable and possibly even looking like anyone. It seems hopeless, and it burns when I consider that perhaps Melanie would be able to figure it out if I were inside a state prison and she were out here.

I wake up later than I expect and have a much clearer head than I did yesterday. It's already after 9 a.m., and my rage is at a low boil, but at least I feel like I have a new day in front of me to do something about it.

When I stumble out of Miles's bedroom in the same clothes of his I wore yesterday, I find him on one of the two stools by his kitchen counter, an empty plate smeared with maple syrup in front of him. The other plate, presumably for me, has a handful of pancakes on it. There's a glass of orange juice next to the plate and a fork on a napkin, like this is a cute diner.

His eyes widen, perhaps because my grogginess is too much like last night's glowering, but with this kind of bountiful breakfast, I really can't be pissy anymore.

I hold up a hand and take a deep breath.

"It's alright," I say. "I'm still angry, but I'm dealing with it. And in case it needs to be said, it's not your fault. In fact, thank you for everything you've done to help."

Miles's big brown eyes soften, and it's like a weight is lifted off his shoulders. I don't know why. At the bottom of it, my problems are not his problems, and I shouldn't be taking his help for granted.

The least I can do is be good company.

But then I sit down on the other stool and smell something odd that's definitely not steaming pancakes or sugary maple syrup.

"Are you wearing cologne?" I ask.

"It's my deodorant," he says, slouching.

"OK."

I slowly take a bite. He's so honest that if he wants to fudge the line on his body spray, he can be my guest without me busting his balls over it, but the smell is kind of strong. Then I look at his hair and can't be entirely sure but suspect he may have combed it. At least the big lick is unusually tame today.

There hasn't been enough time for me to know what he's usually like and what he'd do that's special, but I suspect I may have something to do with it. As I eat, I keep looking him over in search of other things that may be different. Or maybe I do it simply because I like looking at him.

"This is good," I say, either talking about the pancakes or spending time with a man my age who starts the day by actually putting some effort into making our time together nice. Both are novelties for me.

Miles, in a plain white t-shirt and striped boxers, sucks his teeth like it's about to quickly get significantly less good.

"Taylor and Wesley said they'll be over first thing in the morning," he says.

I glance at the door and brace myself for their imminent arrival, but then I kick myself and recall who we're talking about.

It's 11:35 a.m. when the knock comes at the door, and I get up from the couch to answer it, as if I have any right to be greeting people at an apartment that isn't mine. As expected, it's Taylor and Wesley looking like two peas in a pod with furtive grins and plenty of attitude. The only thing they're missing are matching shirts.

"Hi," I say, stepping aside so they can come in.

As they do, Taylor takes a nice long look at me from toes to head before catching my eyes.

"He looks good on you," she says at a volume I hope isn't loud enough for Miles to hear at his computer, and I realize she's talking about his clothes that I'm wearing.

If I'd known where I'd end up, I would've grabbed clothes of my own when I stopped at my apartment yesterday—this is something that'll have to get fixed today, or else I'll keep getting comments like this.

Smiling blandly, I don't bother to confirm or deny anything, and she tilts her head at Wesley like she expects me to ask what they did, and I sure don't do that either.

"You moving in or something?" Wesley asks, and I shake my head but realize the question's gotten Miles's attention.

"We're trying to figure out what to do as quickly as possible," I say. "My parents have a thirty-six-hour head start and could be anywhere in the world doing anything they want with the money they stole."

Wesley bobbles his head a little, clearly looking for a more provocative answer, but moves with Taylor to the couch, where they flop against each other comfortably. Miles swivels around in his computer chair. And that leaves me in the plush recliner, my splayed fingers clutching the ends of the puffy arms like I'm queen of this little court.

Handsome Duke Miles says, "I've spent some time this morning searching for anything that might indicate where Diedre and Martin Marks might have gone, but I can't find anything visible from within the last few days."

Shaking his head, buffoonish rogue Wesley asks, "What, do you think they'd immediately show up somewhere and post a TripAdvisor review under their own names?"

Miles shrugs.

"I thought the whole point of you going to see your sister was that she'd tell you where your parents were," says unrepentant harlot Taylor.

I sigh, having no choice but to give up my royal airs and relive some of the trauma from yesterday.

"She knew plenty about what they were up to but has no idea where they went next or what their plans are now. That makes two of us. Traveling wasn't really my parents' thing. I remember them taking a couple of trips to Vegas and sticking us with relatives. Conceivably, they're trying to find somewhere safe to hide out with their money."

"Without a doubt they've left the country and have moved the money out of the US financial system," Miles says. "Otherwise, they'd always be at risk of getting caught and having everything seized."

"That only leaves every other country in the world," Taylor says.

I shake my head and gently pinch the bridge of my nose. It's easy to let defeatism sink in and figure they're gone for good, but there has to be a way to find them.

"Not really," I say. "They've gone somewhere with a beach, and they don't speak any other languages, so that would cut a lot out."

"Most places you can get away with only speaking English if you want to," Wesley says.

I lean forward, a feeling in my gut guiding me.

"Yeah, but even the prospect of a language barrier would put them off. I keep trying to remember if they have any connection to anywhere they might lean on, but all I keep thinking about is their hunger for luxury. They're not at a beach in the middle of nowhere. They're somewhere where they can get pampered and be as comfortable as humanly possible."

I keep trying to think hard, but I get distracted by Wesley's grumbling.

"Devil's advocate, maybe they're doing something completely different from what you'd expect them to," he says.

"I don't think they're smart enough for something like that."

"They were smart enough to steal hundreds of millions of dollars," Wesley shoots back, causing Taylor to raise her hands.

"Can we stop this? This is starting to sound like another meeting, and if I wanted to have one of those, I'd go back to work," she says. "By the way, have you heard what's going on at Bedrock? The entire company has imploded. Everyone is out of a job, so I guess I have nothing better to do than this."

Wesley leans against her and casts a loving look in her direction.

"Never having to deal with something like that is why it's better not to have a job to begin with."

I roll my eyes, having another moment regretting ever being with him, when Miles saves me from having to scold them.

"I don't think we're looking at this the right way. Purely on the basis of them wanting to protect their money, there are a lot of places they wouldn't want to go. There are few industrialized countries where they wouldn't be at risk," he explains.

I nod along, thinking that's a good point.

"OK, so English speaking, known for ocean-side resorts, and a shady financial system," I say.

Crossing her arms, Taylor doesn't look like any of this is engaging her.

"Let's see. Off the top of my head, English is an official language of the Philippines. Then there's Jamaica, South Africa, and Singapore. I don't think we can rule out Australia or New Zealand, depending on what kind of documentation they could fake. And what about Fiji, the Bahamas, or Papua New Guinea? If they have their hearts set on it, I bet they could find a beach in Switzerland too."

My irritation coming back, I close my eyes and wish I could close my ears long before she's finished. I raise a hand.

"Alright, I get it," I say, and she shrugs.

"All I'm saying is that basically the whole world could be a possibility. There's no way we're going to find them like this. Your best bet is to try to get back into their penthouse and look for some kind of clue that would tell you where they went."

I realize I like Taylor even less when she's trying to be helpful than when she's trying to gaslight me and be condescending.

"I don't have time for that," I say, hurt. "I'd probably get caught by somebody if I went there anyway. I have to find my parents so I can get my sister out of jail, and the answer has to be in front of us. There has to be something we're not thinking of."

Miles shoots me a sympathetic look, and I know what he's about to say isn't going to be comforting.

"But even if we have a good idea, what are we going to do

then? Call the authorities and say we think they're probably in this one particular place with no real evidence? That's not really helpful for them."

Wading in this pressure isn't comfortable, and every time someone says something, it makes it harder for me to keep my head above the surface.

"No," I say, doing my best to stay calm for Melanie's sake, "once we figure out where they are, I go there and physically find them."

"A confrontation," Wesley says, getting excited. "But there's no way you can do that alone. What if they have those FBI guys with them? I'm coming."

Miles glares at Wesley before turning to me.

"They tried to kill you once—"

"Twice," I correct him, "but who's counting?"

He shakes his head. "The point is that trying to directly engage with them under any circumstances is dangerous and would be better off left to professionals."

I look at him and hear the completely reasonable things he's saying. All this talk is making him uncomfortable, and I again worry he's going to figure out that this isn't what he wants to be doing and bolt. One kiss doesn't obligate him to turn his entire life over to me, even if he is suddenly unemployed.

Our eyes connect, and I hope he sees the depth of my commitment.

"No one knows them better than I do or will work as hard as I can. I will find them and make them set this right," I promise, even though I have no idea how.

He purses his lips and scratches his jaw, weighing something in his mind. There are a lot of things I want to say to him, but now's not the time with Taylor and Wesley here. All I can do is wait and hope he has enough faith in me.

"I can't let all of the investors get robbed or your sister stay in jail. But I don't think you see the weight they've placed on you. I want to help," he says, making me feel warm inside.

If it were easy, I don't think it would mean so much, but he's swallowing his doubts for me when his common sense is telling him otherwise. I want to be someone who deserves that kind of selflessness, not a liar dodging a murder rap.

Taylor leans back and puts one leg over the other.

"You know I'll go anywhere with a beach, but all of this is still pointless, because we don't have anything solid to go on about where they went," she says.

Uncomfortable silence fills the room. I don't know what's going through their minds, but I'm trying to recall anything that might help. Scowling, I lean against the side of the chair and replay everything my parents said that night in their office, trying to glean the smallest clue.

Something strikes me, and it's not anything my parents said at all. I sit up, so jazzed that I'm almost shaking.

"That's not true," I say, casting frantic glances around at the others. "We know when they left."

8

Miles is a whiz on his laptop, using all of his fingers to type. It occurs to me that he probably grew up with a computer in his house, perhaps even one in his room.

In seemingly no time at all, he's put together a list of all of the flights that left from Dallas Fort Worth International Airport the night before last when my parents made their heisty departure from the Bedrock Financial building. Yes, "heist" has an adjective form.

The four of us crowd around his screen and analyze the list, which is in columns with the exact takeoff time, plane type, flight number, destination, and flight time.

"Wow, you even removed all of the domestic flights," I cheer, impressed. "Looks like the flights went all over—Tokyo, London, Cairo, Cancún, Quito, Rio, Paris. This list goes on and on. Who knew there were so many flights leaving all the time?"

Although it's a big list, I'm absorbed reading through it and already mentally crossing out ones that wouldn't be likely destinations for my parents. This might be a backdoor way of tracking them down, but I've got a good feeling about my chances, considering what I know about them.

It would be easier having something straightforwardly tell us where they went, but I have no problem putting two and two together to pinpoint the solution.

Except as I glance around to gauge who's sharing my excitement, I realize not everyone sees this equation working out so easily.

An agonized sigh from Taylor is a warning sign about what's coming.

"Do we even know for sure that they took a plane? And how do we know they left from Dallas Fort Worth? Maybe they drove to Houston or something?"

I give her a wearied look.

"Drove to Houston? Come on. They didn't drive anywhere. My parents want everything to be easy and quick. Hours in the car is not part of that. They were talking about needing to leave urgently, and I didn't get any impression that included a long drive," I say.

She shakes her head but doesn't continue to argue. I think I'm in the clear until Wesley starts scratching his chin.

"Devil's advocate again, but maybe they took a connecting flight to somewhere. That's not hard or unusual. There's no guarantee they're still at any of these locations."

That one's harder to bat away, and I glare grimly at Wesley's big chin and hairless collarbone area peeking out from under his t-shirt. I don't want to look him in his blue eyes and admit he might be right.

"First of all, you may not fully understand what devil's advocate means. Second, this is the best we've got and should at least look at the plausible possibilities. Then we can see where they might've gone from there or if that seems like a final destination."

I nod as I explain, hoping some of it gets through. He gives me a placating one in return, which I'm happy to settle for right now if it means we can get closer to finding my parents.

Miles swivels in his chair so that he can face the rest of us. He's got his arms crossed and a studious look on his face. I feel like he's going to start sweet-talking me about retirement accounts and investment portfolios.

"Right, we can screen this through our previous criteria and continue to build segments based on probable destinations. They didn't travel forever and have to trust that their money is following them to the same place. Without any records, there's a degree to which we have to take a leap of faith, but at the same time I think there are only a few realistic possibilities," he explains.

"Which ones?" I ask, eager.

With the push of a button, almost all of the spreadsheet entries vanish, leaving only a few.

We all peer hard at the screen.

"Quito, Ecuador," Wesley reads. "George Town, Cayman Islands. And then the island of Samoa."

Miles glances at the list, seeming to ponder it.

"I'd consider these the most likely because of their proximity to beaches, their banking system, and the potential they have for a couple like the Markses to be able to hide out."

I take one look at the screen and immediately know the answer.

"They went to the Cayman Islands. The other two aren't even close to being likely," I say, getting a feeling in my mouth like I've tasted the answer.

Miles raises an eyebrow at me, and I wonder if I'm about to get an argument from him.

"Let's not jump to any conclusions too quickly. Yes, the Cayman Islands are a notorious tax shelter for wealthy people all around the world, but the other two—"

"No, that's it," I say, my mind made up.

"I agree," Taylor says.

"Case closed," Wesley chimes in.

Our unanimous agreement leads to some grumbling from Miles after we've steamrolled his methodical approach, but I don't need more debate. My parents are there, and I'm one step closer to finding them and setting this straight.

Since the spreadsheet has fully served its purpose, we cease hunching over to stare at the screen and straighten up. A thousand thoughts are stampeding through my head at once about everything I need to do to make this work.

"I need to pack a bag, one filled with my own clothes, preferably," I say.

Wesley opens the fridge and helps himself to a can of Coke.

"Whoa, whoa, whoa, isn't it premature to jump right onto a plane? Even if we know what island they're on, there's still no guarantee we're ever going to actually find them. You said they could be traveling under any name they could think up. And there are how many resorts or hotels in George Town?"

Miles does some swiveling and typing. "Over fifty at least," he says, and Wesley sighs.

Before things can get out of hand, I quickly say, "But how many of those are the kind of high-end resorts my parents would likely stay at? They're not going to set foot in any place that isn't ultra fancy and top of the line. I doubt there are more than a couple of dozen places."

"But their names could be anything," Taylor says. "Unless you physically see them, you'll have no idea where they are. If they're in the room or someplace that's not accessible unless you're actually staying at their particular resort, it could be impossible to spot them."

I take a deep breath, remembering my parents' talk of lounging on the beach, but then a thought strikes me, leading to a broad smirk. Next thing I know, I'm dashing out of the room and into Miles's bedroom, where I've left a few things on the nightstand. Beaming, I trot back in to rejoin the others.

"What did you need in there?" Taylor asks suggestively.

"This," I say, holding up the family picture I retrieved from my desk at Bedrock when Miles started occupying it. "We can use this to show people who we're looking for. My dad has some gray in his hair now, and Mom has some wrinkles, but they still look very much like this."

Taylor and Wesley check out the photo before Miles takes it and puts it in his scanner. A few minutes later, after Miles does some image-editing wizardry, he prints out four much larger versions of the picture, all without taking the original out of the case.

I'm bubbling with excitement when another thought strikes me.

"But there's a chance that if they see me when I'm walking around with this, they'll recognize me. I'll have to put together a different look," I say, wondering what I'd need to do to evade detection.

Wesley and Miles exchange a look. "There goes the afternoon," Wesley says.

Boys...

Miles swivels back around and does some more typing. "Well, that doesn't matter anyway, because the next flight to George Town is another red-eye—tonight, fortunately. And then the next one is a few days after. They have them twice a week."

I would be speechless at how this is coming together if I didn't know exactly what to say.

"That's perfect! Go ahead and book the tickets," I say.

"Alright," Miles says, eyeing me again before he returns his attention to the screen and does some clicking. I'll have to remember to grab my passport. Good thing a short trip I took to Mexico a few years ago means I have one.

The clicking noticeably stops, and I focus on Miles.

"What's wrong?" I ask.

"So how many nights are we staying?" he asks as he searches for tickets, though I get the sense that this isn't what's bothering him.

"Probably a week to look through all these places," Wesley says, making Miles's eyes widen.

"We'll have this wrapped up in two nights," I counter, champing at the bit to get going.

Next to me, Taylor scoffs. "There's no way it'll be that quick, and I'll hardly be able to work up a good tan by then."

"Better just plan to take the next flight back," Miles decides, punching it in. I quickly agree, though in my head I vow to stay there as long as it takes, all the while trying not to think about what would happen if they up and left quickly.

But they were going somewhere to relax and lie low where the US authorities can't get them. There's no chance they take off unless they're spooked, which gets me to look at my reflection in the window and think about how I can avoid doing that.

A long sigh from Miles draws my attention back.

"Is there a problem?" I ask, and for once he's not quick to answer and doesn't shift back to look at me.

I glance over his shoulder at the screen and get the sense that the tickets are all in the cart and Miles has made it to the checkout screen. Looks good to me.

I flew on a plane once when I was part of an elementary school chorus group, but not since then, so even the prospect of getting in an airplane is thrilling. I find it hard to believe that Miles's enthusiasm is plummeting.

"Nothing is a problem, per se. Everything is queued up and ready to go, but there's one question remaining."

I wait for him to go on and say what it is, but he doesn't. "Which is what?"

"So how is this getting paid for?"

Typical me neglecting to remember that doing big things like chasing my parents around the world will cost money. My mouth is hanging open, and all I can do is lean to the side to take another look at the screen. Last-minute round-trip tickets for the four of us are over five grand, and then there's all the expenses we haven't even considered.

My bank account hasn't change since Hochatown, meaning I can barely afford a tank of gas.

"I'm flat broke," Wesley scoffs, and when I turn to Taylor, she's already lowered her eyes at me.

"I thought you said we'd be paid to help, not to mention free airfare," she says, leaning back.

I glare at her.

"I didn't say anything at all like that. You know I didn't," I say, and she crosses her arms and cocks her head at me.

"But it would make sense though, right? I don't have a job anymore, you can't do this alone, and we can't do this for nothing."

Shaking my head, I realize I don't have time for another battle over who said what when or what everyone is supposed to get out of this.

"Just say you don't have the money to pay, Taylor. A trip to the Caribbean has to be enough on its own, and you better seriously help find them and do whatever else needs to be done," I say, and she groans.

"I've *been* helping. What do you think I've been doing here this whole time? You wouldn't have even figured out where they might be if not for me. So are you paying, or what?"

My indignation that she'd try to profit off my search quickly gets buried beneath the cold reality of the costs involved.

"I can't pay for this," I say meekly, sulking. "Alice might have the money, but this would be major theft putting it on her card. It's not an option."

That only leaves one of us left, and I shift to Miles with a pitiful expression on along with his flannel shirt and jeans. I can't bring myself to say what everyone expects me to say, leading to a painful, uncomfortable smile that definitely can't be turning him on.

"If they've made it out of the country, they could seriously get away with everything," he says in a low voice, almost like he's already trying to talk himself into it.

I wring my hands in front of my waist. The big price tag is there on the screen, only the beginning of the expenses the four of us would rack up over two nights or however long it takes.

Suddenly I recall how it felt when Alice and Taylor turned on me in Hochatown and told me that I was going to have to pay for everything. Now I'm voluntarily putting Miles into my shoes, which have to be tight and pinching. There's no other way, and I have to believe it'll be good for him doing this for me.

There's the temptation to argue that this could be even bigger than the time he saved all of those H&R Block customers, but that won't sway him. What matters is us.

"Please, Miles."

He gives me a long look, torn. I don't know how much money he has after being in private school, but I don't get the impression that this is chump change.

"Is this about revenge?" he asks me.

I answer solemnly, "Sometimes revenge and justice are two sides of the same coin."

Slowly, the tension around his brown eyes fades, giving him a tranquil look I wish I could feel. He reaches over to the laptop and clicks to purchase the tickets.

A success screen thanking him for his order pops up, and

suddenly Wesley, Taylor, and I are cheering. I clap and dance, setting a hand on Miles's shoulder and hoping I don't owe him too much for putting himself out there for me.

Enjoying our enthusiasm, Miles grins despite himself.

"My parents are going to kill me for this," he says.

I wave my hand.

"It's not as bad as you'd think."

9

My hair is covered in enough sludgy black goop that it looks like I've dipped my head in an oil spill.

As the clock ticks and I say goodbye to my dirty-blond hair color, I hope this change buys me some anonymity and peace of mind when I inevitably find my parents. There's this perception that blondes have more fun, but that certainly hasn't been true over the past few days.

The stylist goes through all of the steps, brushing the thick dye on every strand, wrapping it all in plastic, and now washing out the excess product with my head dipped back into a big sink.

When I'd walked in, I'd told her point-blank, "I have this much money and need to look completely different in two hours. What can you do?"

The time is up, and she spins me around to look at myself in the mirror, standing a little off to the side with a raised eyebrow. My hair is dark brown and on the shorter side with bangs, and my first thought is that I've turned into my sister.

After moonlighting as Alice, the last thing I want is to be any different from what I am, but the idea of channeling my incarcerated sister as I take down our parents has definite appeal.

They won't recognize me, and they won't expect her since she's been in prison for five years, but a part of Melanie will be with me when I do this for her.

"What do you think?" the stylist, Jamie, asks.

"Miraculous!" I say.

She even touches up my face, my bruise quickly fading away now that most of a week has gone by. It's nice feeling like a real person again, and seeing myself with this kind of look makes me feel daunting and relentless.

I hope Miles doesn't mind it.

Once I pay Jamie, I leave the salon and head to my apartment to pack up and get ready to go. There's still a lot to do before the flight to George Town, but since money is scarce, bikini shopping isn't on the list. Miles will have to settle for seeing me in my faded old two-pieces.

The walk to my apartment gives me plenty of time to have serious qualms about this trip, not least of all because it's uncomfortably close to scamming Miles. He wants to be the hero for truth and all of the people Bedrock has ripped off, but I can't pretend to care about them too much.

What I want is to free my sister and get back at my parents for ruining our lives. The pain of the last ten years thinking my sister was dead even outweighs watching a bullet zip by millimeters from my head a couple of nights ago.

For all the blood-pumping zeal I have to chase them down, I'm also secretly afraid it won't work out and will lead to something worse. Mom had a grand scheme that took years to pull off to build a huge investment firm to steal millions of dollars. My sister orchestrated a way to get me to stop them from prison far away.

The thing I can't admit to anybody is that I have no clue what I'm going to do to get what I want. I go to George Town. I find my parents. Something happens. They end up in jail, my sister is freed, and all of the stolen money gets returned.

That's a big gap in the plan.

My discomfort seems to echo my increasingly achy feet, and by the time I get to my dingy apartment building, I feel like I'll collapse on the steps.

I can't remember the last time I paid my rent and am half expecting to find an eviction notice on my door, but instead the coast is clear and I cruise inside my apartment to the mess I'd left behind.

Bare mattress on the floor next to some Chinese food containers. Nearly empty refrigerator. The three-legged table still has an application on it for a part-time, minimum-wage job at a youth center, my fallback in case things didn't work out with Bedrock.

More than the clutter, the cramped apartment has a persistent smell of mildew that no amount of Febreze can get rid of.

And I'd had to fight hard to make it into this apartment after being in transient housing after being homeless and crashing at friends' places. And sometimes they weren't even friends.

First, I change out of Miles's clothes, opting for a pair of light-gray cotton shorts and a teal athletic tech top. It's nice to be able to take a full breath without worrying that I'm going to pop a button off his flannel shirt.

The closest thing to luggage I have is the backpack I used in high school, the same bag I'd taken to Hochatown, and I get to work trying to stuff it with everything I'll need for a four-day trip.

Between basic hygiene items and clothes, the bag fills up quickly and isn't going to leave me with many options of what to wear while I'm there. The best I can do to try to fudge the issue is to put on a second layer over what I'm already wearing.

Although we've got the larger printed images, I keep the

family portrait with me as well as the ten-thousand-dollar bonus check written out to Alice for my death, my first one. If there were a chance Bedrock still had any money left, I would be sorely tempted to cash it to relieve Miles of the burden of paying for everything, but it's one of the few tangible items related to what's going on, and I need to keep it with me.

It's only late afternoon by the time I'm fully packed, and even after raiding my cupboard and finding some old oatmeal and buried beef jerky that may even be from a previous tenant, there are hours and hours remaining before I need to meet the others at the airport.

But I cast a dissatisfied look around the apartment and decide I'd rather leave right away regardless, even if it would be nominally more comfortable here than the hard plastic chairs at the airport.

Backpack on, I close the door behind me as I step out into the hall and start toward the stairwell, expecting another long walk through Dallas in which I sink into my thoughts and avoid the outside world as much as possible.

Right as I'm about to open the door to the stairwell, it pulls open away from me of its own accord, and I'm suddenly facing a large man with a thick mustache and a big light-brown hat. He's got a matching uniform on, and I immediately recognize him.

He's the McCurtain County sheriff, the one who found me by the lake in Hochatown and then called me on Alice's cell phone.

Stifling the urge to panic, I try to keep my face blank and simply continue on my way around him as he steps into the hall with me. But of course he notices me, since I'm right there in front of him.

"Excuse me," he says firmly and loudly enough that it's impossible for me to pretend I didn't hear him.

I have no choice but to stop and wash my eyes over him as if I have no idea who he is or what he's doing here.

"Yeah," I say with as little energy as I can, every ounce of my focus on keeping myself placid and detached instead of shocked and petrified.

He looks me over for a second and then glances down the hallway.

"Do you know a girl named Emily Marks?" he asks.

I squint at him and shake my head. No, I have no idea who that girl is, who she might have killed, and where she might be running to. All I can think about is that I'll never find my parents if I'm suddenly arrested and forced to stand up Miles, Taylor, and Wesley at the airport.

"Who? Sorry, I don't," I say, trying to make my voice a little gruffer.

I turn away quickly but hopefully not so fast that it makes him think I'm running away from him.

"Wait," he says, and I stop and wince hard, one foot in the stairwell and my back to him. "What are you doing here?"

"Visiting my boyfriend."

I glance over my shoulder at the sheriff and raise a shoulder, gesturing to my backpack, as if that's evidence of anything.

A second passes, and that's all the go-ahead I need to start moving again, and I hold my breath until I hear the door close behind me. Then once I'm a few steps down and turning out of sight from the window, I bolt the rest of the way until I'm at the ground floor and able to dart out onto the street.

The sheriff's cruiser is parked right there on the street in the middle of Dallas, quite a ways away from McCurtain County, Oklahoma. It must be slow over there if this guy came all this way himself. Why can't we all just forget Alice ever existed?

I start speed walking away and don't even glance at the cruiser long enough to see if the dumb deputy I'd lied to about being Alice is sitting inside. Thank goodness I didn't pass him on the way down, but being inches away from the sheriff was bad enough.

Alice's death continues to be really inconvenient for me when I have so many more important things to do with my living and breathing body. It's almost enough to make me regret taking Taylor's knife-wielding hand and guiding it to Alice's chest, after Alice attempted to kill me while performing a hit job orchestrated by my parents.

And why doesn't the sheriff figure out enough to go after Taylor instead? If she didn't show up to the airport in time for the flight to George Town, I wouldn't shed a tear about it.

I get far enough away from the cruiser that I start to relax and think the coast is clear. No plans to ever return to my apartment again now that the sheriff is on to me, I wonder how long and how far I'll have to run to get away from this investigation for good.

But the long walk to Dallas Fort Worth International Airport takes on a different tone when I realize that Miles could never be with someone who avoids responsibility and has to lie about who she is.

He's spending thousands of dollars, flying to a place he's never been, and upending his life to right other people's wrongs, and I can't even tell the truth about my own name a few feet from my door because of the things I've done.

It makes me wonder what I'll have to do to keep him and when he'll catch on to what my life is really like—hopefully not during a couple days on white sandy beaches in a Caribbean paradise.

I reach the airport and spend another hour sitting near the entrance as I wait for the others to arrive. Taylor and Wesley arrive five minutes before Miles, all of them full of excitement and with big smiles.

It takes some work to bury my unease about my unexpected but predictable brush with the law so that I can turn up my own enthusiasm.

"This is going to be so much fun!" I say, even going so far as to set a hand on Taylor's shoulder. "Nothing like a few days of sun, surf, and scam busting!"

Taylor laughs and then touches my hair.

"And you make such a brilliant brunette! If I cut my hair, I could pass as you," she says.

"Let's not try that," I chuckle, my eyes flitting to Miles to see if he's picked up on our topic of conversation.

His expression is pleasant enough, but he's not over the moon about anything, whether it's the trip or my hair. I wonder if his misgivings are still weighing on him, or maybe he prefers me as a sandy blonde.

"Let's not waste any time. Even if we can find them, we don't know how long they'll stay in one place," he says.

I nod soberly, remembering that my time for coming up with an incredible plan is growing even shorter. And I have a feeling it'll have to be much better than pretending that the car won't start.

"I call aisle seat. Gotta stretch out," Wesley says in a sleeveless tank top and khaki shorts, looking the part at least.

I roll my eyes.

"I think the tickets assign our seats," I say.

"Yeah, but we can switch," he says.

We move on through security, and I'm glad it's only the McCurtain County sheriff asking after me and not Dallas PD or the FBI with an official arrest warrant, because then I'd never make it past TSA to get on the flight. But I breeze through without trouble, and after some more waiting and carousing we're given the green light to board.

Stepping onto the smallish aircraft with my ticket in hand, it turns out I have an aisle seat and happily give it up to Wesley, which puts me on the opposite side next to Miles, even if I am squeezed into a middle seat. The plane starts rolling and gets in position for takeoff.

The four of us glance at each other across the aisle and laugh, like this is one big double-date vacation with nothing more planned than lounging on the beach, cocktails, and fooling around once we're behind our separate closed doors.

I must not've been the only one to have thoughts of our accommodations cross my mind, because Wesley asks, "So which of these resorts are we staying at anyway?"

I immediately get a picture in my head of infinity pools, room service, and incredible ocean views under a star-speckled sky.

Miles chuckles, shrugging.

"After what these tickets cost, it won't be a fancy resort, but I did find a great place for us," he says, as if that should settle the matter.

But I've picked up on his tension and can't let this go.

"Where?"

He glances at me with a big grin, like everything will be perfectly fine.

"You'll love it. It's an Airbnb."

Taylor and I couldn't have jerked forward faster if the plane came to a sudden stop. We exchange a look of mortified dread.

The plane accelerates for takeoff, but I look for the emergency exit.

Airbnb? Oh no! Is it too late for me to jump out?

10

A red-eye flight means another night of poor sleep, and shortly after takeoff they dim the cabin lights and let people doze as best they can.

I sense Miles is able to check out pretty easily, perhaps because he's used to flying on planes, but the gentle hum of the engine erases any chance of me nodding off. The seat isn't nearly as comfortable as Miles's bed, but I can hear him breathing softly next to me, which is a plus.

It's almost like we're sleeping together, except there are probably a hundred other people around, and I'm not sleeping.

Figuring I can sleep when I'm dead, I take advantage of this quiet time to get to work on my amazing but so-far-nonexistent plan to catch my parents and make them free my sister. Once I find them, I'll threaten to sic the CIA on them if they don't confess to the crime Melanie is in jail for.

No, that'll never work. They'd call my bluff about calling the authorities and would die before confessing or admitting to anything. I'll have to think of another way that doesn't involve needing their cooperation, but right now I'm still drawing a blank.

My mental gymnastics trying to work out a solution gets rudely interrupted when a flight attendant starts walking down the aisle. A lady in her forties with her hair up and a lot of makeup, the usual crisp uniform, slowly creeps along, seemingly checking on everybody to see if they're asleep.

It's difficult to ignore any movement or distraction in the darkened cabin, and I watch her out of my half-closed eyes and wait for her to pass us on her way to someplace in the back of the plane.

Right as she's about to pass our row, I see a hand go up to halt her from the aisle seat on the other side.

"Hey, Miss," Wesley whispers loudly enough for me to hear. I wince, wondering if he's going to flirt with her right in front of Taylor, asleep beside him. "Is there champagne on this flight?"

My head turns to the side to be able to watch, though I'm tucked in behind Miles. I gawk at Wesley, who surely could've asked for water if he's thirsty. The attendant seems unsure of how to react as well.

"There's no drink service now," she says.

"But there is for the right price, isn't there?"

Wesley responds within a fraction of a second, quicker than it takes me to wonder why he'd be splurging on booze during a red-eye flight after complaining that he couldn't pay for his own ticket.

Oh, duh. I almost slap myself on the forehead, giving away that I'm awake. I start to move, sensing that I need to get in the middle of this, but the attendant's back is to me, and she starts talking before I can so much as move a muscle.

"I'll make it happen," she says, starting off.

"Be sure to charge it to the seat," Wesley adds smugly, seeming to relax as he faces forward and waits for her to return with his drink.

The damage is done before I can so much as make a peep,

and I glare at the faintly visible part of Wesley I can see from my angle.

Now I'm the one breathing heavily. I just witnessed Wesley stealing from Miles not two feet away from him, and I can only imagine how Miles will react when he discovers that additional charge on his card.

But as much as I'm angry on behalf of Miles, I'm even more disappointed in Wesley. Writing off the iPod swipe as a momentary mistake was more than he deserved, and I have to acknowledge I'd been duped again by his pleas that he would change and give up the bad behavior.

Now we're all doing this together, and he's going to be in the thick of it with us. I should've listened to Miles's warnings on the drive to the women's prison. No matter what plans I come up with, there's a risk that Wesley won't be able to avoid screwing it all up when his own interests get in the way.

Moments later, he has a slim flute in his hand that has a golden shine as it catches a narrow overhead light. The urge to breathe fire hits as he takes sips and swirls the glass, but Miles is sleeping like a baby next to me. I can't wake him up, but I know I'll find a way to make sure Wesley pays Miles back for the drink.

The flight to Grand Cayman is nearly four hours, and I spend most of it stewing and trying to think of how I can manage Wesley and keep him from ruining everything we have going for us. Deep down, I'm afraid that Miles will blame me when Wesley or Taylor step out of line.

Only the sight of the island in the early-morning light snaps me out of my inconvenient pessimism. A tropical paradise of palm trees, sandy beaches, and resorts seems to jut out of the sea on this flat expanse of land. Screens in the backs of the seats in front of us say that the island is seventy-five square miles and twenty-two miles long. The population of George Town is about thirty-five thousand, and I lean closer to the window feeling like I can already spot two occupants in particular.

The plane starts its approach, and I succumb to a growing certainty that my parents are down there, helpless in the face of my tenacious effort to find them. My life depends on making Diedre and Marty Marks pay for what they've done, and it's a good thing I have the element of surprise going for me, since they think I'm dead.

The plane seems to wobble a lot as we descend to the runway. The landing is so rocky that we're all giving each other uneasy smiles of relief by the time the plane comes to a stop. That plus more than the four hours of flight time gives us a sense of urgency to disembark, and I for one feel nervous butter-flies as the procession of occupants slowly inches down the aisle toward the door leading outside.

Even though I didn't sleep at all, I'm full of nervous energy that leaves me bouncing on my toes, itching to get outside and start looking.

"You have a good rest?" Wesley asks Miles with a friendly grin that only I know is full of it.

"Could've been worse," Miles says.

"I slept fine too," Taylor says, clearly annoyed that she wasn't asked.

Wesley leans against her shoulder. "I know you did. You were right next to me."

I'm hardly paying attention to them when we're nearly off the plane, fresh air and freedom now only feet away. The flight attendant with her hair up gives me a tepid smile before bright-ening up significantly for Wesley behind me, but I couldn't care less and slip through the opening.

The first thing that hits me is the warm, humid air with a light ocean breeze. The soft morning sun feels like a gentle caress, and from the top of the stairs I catch glimpses of the Caribbean all around us.

Once we're all down and walking to the airport gate, I can hardly contain my excitement.

"This is incredible! Everything here feels so fresh and pure. This is already like a beautiful dream," I say, ogling some flowers by the terminal and the seabirds floating lazily overhead.

Miles raises an eyebrow at me. "Yes, the Cayman Islands are known for their enchanting combination of pristine beaches and tax evasion."

I purse my lips, thinking I'm being teased, even if he is right.

Taylor speaks up on the other side of him, "Come for the surf, stay for dodging accountability to your own government."

I'm in such a good mood and don't mind snickering at her comment along with Miles, but it's a good reminder of why my parents surely came here in the first place. Every person I see around the airport terminal could be my parents and needs to be inspected, and I wonder if I'll still be in high spirits when I finally spot them.

After grabbing some snacks that'll pass for our breakfast, we have the entire morning in front of us before we can check in at the Airbnb. That gives us plenty of time to get started on our search.

"In addition to the enlarged photos of Mom and Dad that Miles made, I've taken the liberty of assigning us each five of the twenty fanciest hotels here. We can get started while we're waiting to check in. Take your list, ask at the front desk using the photo, and then look around as much as possible. Since it's the morning, be sure to hit any dining rooms during breakfast service."

I had scribbled lists of hotels on napkins and hand them out to the others. The part I don't share with them is that I've saved the five most likely choices for myself. Taylor and Wesley could easily get distracted or just plain give up early, while Miles might not recognize my parents even if he is staring right at them, family photo or not.

Taylor cringes at her napkin like I've asked her to wipe something up with it.

"This is more organized than I've seen you be about anything. If I didn't know any better, I'd say you put some actual work into this," she says.

I laugh to paper over the embarrassing implication that I'm incapable of doing work. "Yeah, it's too bad there's no way to turn helping people avoid being scammed into a job," I say.

As soon as it's out of my mouth, lightning strikes. A job. Finding my parents is part one, but then after that getting close to them is the next step. Working would be a perfect reason to get close to them, as long as it's not so close that they recognize me, brunette or not.

Miles scratches his chin as he continues to stare at the napkin. I'm tempted to tell him he can take it with him and doesn't have to memorize it.

"But how am I supposed to get into any of these places if I'm not staying at them?" he asks.

Wesley tries to stifle a smirk and fails, breaking out into laughter.

"Dude, you just walk in and start looking around. Act like you belong there."

Cringing back, Miles says, "What if somebody asks me what I'm doing or if I'm a guest?"

"Then you tell them whatever you think will get them to stop bothering you. If you set foot in a hotel, then you can consider yourself a guest," Taylor says with a smile, remarkably free from condescension or spite.

But Miles shakes his head. "A hotel guest is someone who's reserved a room, and I'm not going to make something up to get rid of someone. If I'm not supposed to be somewhere, I shouldn't go in there in the first place," he says.

I set my hand on Miles's shoulder to draw him away from those two and give him a sympathetic close-lipped smile.

"No one's asking you to lie about what you're doing, Miles. You can tell anybody who approaches you what you're doing and who you're looking for. They'll probably try to help you. You're not going to get in trouble or get thrown out, no matter where you go," I say.

It seems to me that should satisfy his need to be honest, but the skeptical look he has erases my confidence. Wesley appears disturbed by Miles's ethics, and Taylor is taking a lot of pleasure in the conversation for some reason.

I sigh, thinking I'll have to take Miles's list of hotels on the second round if he's too skittish to really get in anywhere and look around.

I see the airport terminal's exit doors ahead, but none of the others seem that anxious to get going. As usual, it's going to be up to me, in this case to both find my parents and get the others on their feet so they can go through the motions of helping.

"Hey, the sooner we find them, the sooner we can start to relax and enjoy ourselves, but there's even more in it for you if that's not enough motivation. Whoever finds my parents gets a special reward from me," I declare, standing up first.

Since I'm completely sure that I'll find them myself, I'm more than happy to offer a bribe to make things a little more interesting. It perks Wesley up, at least.

"What is it?" he asks, and I try to avoid grumbling at having to actually come up with something.

"I'll customize something really great for the one who finds them," I say brightly, but Wesley frowns and tilts back in his seat, looking like he has no intention of moving.

"So basically you have no idea and will try to make up something on the spot later," he scoffs, shaking his head.

I glare at Wesley long and hard, unsurprised he'd try to flake out of helping as soon as he'd been flown here. Even if the odds are low, I won't mind at all if Wesley actually finds my parents, but one thing he definitely won't be doing is bringing the rest of us down with shenanigans and a negative attitude.

Some of us don't need a bribe so much as a warning.

"How about this to treat the winner? On the flight back, I'll spring for a glass of champagne."

His eyes widen, and suddenly Wesley's much more keen about getting out of here to start, albeit mostly to avoid my wrath.

11

It's a relief when we set out separately to canvas the island for my parents, both to have the chance to enjoy this magical paradise and to clear my head after some bickering and whining started to set in.

We really need to get this show on the road before the wheels fall off our quartet. Wesley seems ready to flake out at a moment's notice. Taylor's negative attitude is getting tiresome. And now that we're here, I'm definitely not in the mood for any overt displays of virtuousness from Miles when he needs to go do what we came here for.

Once again, I feel like I'm the only one I can really count on, and I'd better find a way to get this done by myself.

It's not too complicated. I have the picture with my parents, my list of five hotels, and my two feet. With some perseverance and luck, I'm hopeful that'll be all I'll need.

George Town is on the west end of the island, which is occupied in large part by the airport. All I need to do is walk up and down the north and sound ends of Church Street, which runs along the coast and connects all of the major hotels on my list.

Sunshine Suites, Hilton, Wyndham, Marriott, and The Ritz-

Carlton are my targets, thanks to sorting the resorts by which ones have the most expensive rooms.

As I trek along the pale-white sidewalk, it's hard not to feel like I'm strolling through a dream. All I have to do is look left to see the ocean with all of its green and blue shades stretching out to the horizon. The waves gently lap against the shore, and I feel like I want to immerse myself in all of it.

Here on dry land, it's not bad either—hardly any traffic on this island, a fair number of tourists strolling about, and cute shops interspersed between the resorts with breathtakingly decadent accommodations. The sun is climbing the morning sky, and the clock is ticking to find my parents.

I scan every single face that passes me, but I know my odds of seeing them out on the street are going to be low. The sun on the sign for Sunshine Suites beckons me, and I pass by some valets milling around the entrance to embrace the blissful air conditioning once inside. The lobby has a crystal chandelier and marble-tiled floor leading to the front desk, but I take Wesley's suggestion and decide to do some snooping on my own first.

Few are out by the pool, a tour through the hallways doesn't turn anyone up, and they're not at the breakfast buffet, where no one would've stopped me if I wanted to help myself to a few things.

It's not long before I accept that I'm not going to bump into them on my own. My only hope is that someone at the desk will give them away.

"Hi, can you tell me if you've seen my friends around? They're supposed to be meeting me here," I say to a pudgy guy in his thirties with red eyes that suggest it's way too early in the morning for him.

But he hops to as soon as I speak, setting his hands on his computer.

"What are their names?" he asks the obvious question, one I'm prepared for.

"That's the thing. They like to play this game where they check in under different names to enhance the experience. I do have this picture of them though, and their real names are Martin and Diedre Marks. Have you seen them?"

I'd folded the picture horizontally so that me and Melanie are hidden, and the clerk takes a long look at the picture but ends up cringing and shaking his head.

"I haven't seen anyone like that, and we don't have anyone with the name Marks here," he says.

I thank him and cut my losses, embarking upon the next leg of my journey up to Hampton by Hilton, which immediately gives me an underwhelming impression based on the bland, cream-colored facade and typical-looking in-ground pool surrounded by beach chairs. I do some looking around and show my photo to a couple of people, but I quickly give up and move on.

Reaching Wyndham after two more miles of walking, my lack of sleep and lengthy trekking are starting to catch up with me, but this resort is on an impressive little peninsula and appears to be a much better candidate.

The bright-blue roof above grand balconies gives off a very pleasing aesthetic, and the multiple tide-pool-style pools in front of a long beach with a pier and inviting waters brings to mind exactly what I pictured when Mom said back in her office that she wanted to be lounging by the beach.

I cruise through the lobby with renewed vigor, enticed by the views and the strong possibility that my parents would choose to stay here, but before I can get to the back doors leading to the waterfront, a voice calls out, "Hey, you!"

I turn with a smile, holding the straps of my backpack.

"Oh, sorry," I say, "I'm just checking out but forgot my sandals by one of the lounge chairs. I'll be right back, alright?"

He begrudgingly lets me go, and I'm thankful Miles isn't in my shoes right now, but a thorough scan of the waterfront from end to end comes up with nothing. I take some extra time to scope out the balconies and then ask several employees about my picture, but there is nothing to go on here.

If this is a game of hot and cold, all I can think is that this place is ice cold.

After bitterly leaving Wyndham, my next stop is the Marriott, which gives me even more of an unlikely feeling than the Hilton. I'm sure the views from the top floor are nice, but the space by the waterfront is this cramped paved deck that goes right up against the water. Not a grain of sand to be found. The tourists, though looking better than many of the people I know in Dallas, don't have that decadent vibe my parents are going for.

Before I know it, I've crossed off another hotel from my list, leaving only one more.

Even before I can see the sign for The Ritz-Carlton, I can tell where I'm headed. With terraced red-tiled roofing, majestic towers set at different heights, and an elaborate resort facade that could be a grand palace for a king, it seems like the entire island is a warm-up act for this ostentatious display of regal splendor.

Even the ruby-red decorative walkway leading into the entrance makes me question whether I'm worthy of walking into such a place. I have to take a deep breath before I press on and go inside, feeling like if my parents aren't here, they aren't anywhere on this island.

The smartly uniformed staff at the entryway certainly notice me but don't stop me longer than it takes to say hi. That in itself is both impressive and a relief. It doesn't feel like they have to bother wringing every dollar they can out of travelers, which is good because I don't have much money.

Touring the building is almost enough to make me forget what I'm doing here. The restaurant decor looks enticing, the amenities are plentiful, and the ocean-side of the resort is like its own perfect world, where not another building can be seen, leaving only a vast stretch of white-sand beach and canopy umbrellas looming over lounge chairs.

I walk slowly and take a careful look at each and every face. I don't see my parents here right now, but I do see so many happy, smiling faces that I have to wonder what life is like for the people wealthy enough to visit here.

Families with young kids frolic in the wading pools. Young adults gather for drinks at the cabana. Some older folks are playing a game of volleyball in another pool, laughing and splashing.

It's so beautiful, a picture of humanity free from stress and pain, that it hurts.

Suddenly, I feel something against my hip as I'm standing on the deck looking out over the waterfront and the vast, immaculate ocean beyond. Startled, I look down to find a little girl, probably six or seven years old, in a cute floral swimsuit with swim goggles making marks on her forehead.

"You dropped this," she says, and I blink when I realize she's holding out a pair of rose-tinted sunglasses, rectangular shaped with a gilded edge along the temples.

"Oh, that's not mine," I blurt out before thinking, causing the girl to run off and give them to a staff member.

It strikes me that I'd seen those glasses before in a magazine or something, and they were Versaces that had to cost over five hundred bucks. Someone had lost track of them and seemingly moved on without them.

A deep breath was required after thinking about how I've

had to scrimp and admittedly take advantage of others to get by, but I don't regret missing the chance to lie and take the glasses for myself. The Versace sunglasses simply aren't mine, and it feels good not to lie to get the things I have.

My search for my parents continues, and I explore the interior and exterior of the resort so thoroughly that it draws some awkward looks from people as I'm checking to make sure of their identities.

"I'm here to meet my friends. Have you seen them?" I ask the staff at the desk, showing off my picture. The young lady with long blond hair behind the counter appears to be my age, and she takes a quick look and then pushes her lips to the side. Her name tag reads, "Sadie."

"I'm not sure," she says, shrugging. Noticing how happy she appears to be at her job, I thank her and step aside.

Although I'm confident they have to be here, my failure to find my parents causes some anxiety to swell up in my chest. Walking faster and trying to keep calm, I stalk the corridors and walkways until I feel like I've crisscrossed the entire place twice.

They aren't here.

The morning has slipped away, and I still haven't found Mom and Dad. It crosses my mind that they could be cloistered in their room straight through to lunch, but I don't believe it. They wanted the sun and the beach and the ocean breeze sweeping through their hair.

My lip quivers as I realize that it's very nearly time for me to start walking to the Airbnb to meet with Miles, Wesley, and Taylor, but I can't seem to pull myself away from this place. Even if I don't feel entitled to so much as sit in a chair, simply standing here on the deck feels like a priceless treasure.

Then, in the midst of oscillating between appreciating how far I've come and loathing my life in the face of all of this, I see something out along the beach.

I quickly realize it's a couple strolling from far out along the stretch of sand, the waves gently lapping at the shore beside them as they walk hand in hand.

My feet start moving before I even realize what I'm doing, and I hurry to get into a better position where I can see them but they can't see me, next to a cluster of palm trees and elephant ears by the end of the resort's deck.

I recognize my mother's wingtips first. She's in a loose white skirt and forest-green sleeveless top. Dad's smile shines white and bright even against the bleached sand and full sunlight.

They're coming this way after a long morning walk out on the beach, bare feet sinking into the loose grains of sand. Dad says something, and Mom laughs, stumbling enough to make her reach out and hold his arm with both of hers.

It's the most romantic thing I've ever seen, a mature man and woman deeply in love enjoying a picturesque promenade along the beach beside the Caribbean after orchestrating a yearslong investment scheme to defraud legions of people out of hundreds of millions of dollars.

Even though I'm standing still and hidden, my heart is pounding in my chest at the sight of them and the recognition that they're staying here at The Ritz-Carlton.

I wait for them to enter the resort's interior before following them in and heading back to that girl at the desk. We have some more business to discuss.

Because it's not enough that I've found Mom and Dad. Now I have to catch them.

12

After a walk of about two miles, I arrive at Canal Street ten minutes late, but I feel like I'm in a state of bliss and have this whole thing in the bag. I found my parents and only need to get enough dirt on them to make them help get Melanie released.

Considering they are buried up to their necks in dirt, how hard can that be?

But despite being late to arrive at our Airbnb for check-in, I'm still the first one here, giving me a few minutes alone to stare uneasily at the building where we'll be staying, part of a long structure running unbroken the entire length of the short side street.

With a two-story plaster facade that appears more like it would fit in along a strip mall than in the vicinity of high-end resorts, it has baby-blue shutters on some second-story windows and thin columns supporting a large awning. The aluminum-framed glass door gives me the impression that this is actually a repurposed storefront.

Other than the address number, there's no signage of any kind indicating what the place is for, and I feel crestfallen after witnessing what goes on at some of the lavish resorts I saw. No one will be dropping any five-hundred-dollar sunglasses around here.

As I'm staring reluctantly at the building, decorated only by some potted palms and a waving Cayman Islands flag, Miles strolls onto Canal Street with Wesley and Taylor together shortly behind.

If I hadn't found my parents on my own, seeing the two of them show up next to each other at the same time would've made me blow a gasket, suggesting they really didn't bother to look that much.

At least Miles has the decency to look glum, and I decide that my good news would be best deployed as a nice surprise once we're out of the sun and comfortably enjoying ourselves.

"Any luck?" I ask with a long face.

Miles purses his lips and shakes his head.

"They're not at the places on my list," he says, sighing. "I looked everywhere I possibly could."

"I know you did your best, and I really appreciate it," I say, putting my hand on his shoulder.

Turning my attention, I notice Taylor has some sand around her collarbone, making me wonder if she did nothing more than find a spot at the beach to hang out.

"I saw someone who looked a lot like your mom at one of the places," Taylor says. "I'll need to go back and try to examine her more thoroughly."

It startles Wesley when he realizes we're all waiting for him to report. "Nobody had seen them, and I couldn't find them anywhere," he says. "Most of the time I was doubting if they'd even come to this island."

I nod sympathetically, not going to be too hard on anybody for failing after most of their places weren't likely targets to begin with.

"I'm so grateful for all of you for doing what you could straight off the plane like that. How about we check in and relax?"

The idea of a break from the sun and heat gets a favorable response, but when it dawns on them where we'd arrived, I'm not the only one who's concerned.

"Is this really where we're staying?" Wesley moans. "I can't even see the water from here. I didn't know that was possible anywhere on this island."

Miles narrows his eyes at him.

"I didn't see you jumping up to try to make last-minute reservations. I'm sure it's not that bad," he says.

"It can't be worse than the last Airbnb we stayed at," Taylor says, taking a deep breath and seeming to steel herself as we start toward the front door.

"As long as the host doesn't end up dead," I say under my breath.

"What was that?" Miles asks.

"Nothing. Cute shutters!" I say, pulling the front door open for them.

We stream into the interior, where there's a pedestal fan oscillating back and forth but nobody in sight, only lime-green tile and a long counter bisecting the space, which had to have been used for some kind of store or possibly even a take-out restaurant. There are lots of cat decorations but no sign of any real cat, some wicker chairs lining a wall, and a fish tank full of cichlids on the other side.

"Hello? Is anybody here?" Miles calls out to no response.

After what we went through with Mr. Chambers in Hocha-town, a part of me really appreciates not having the host be all over us as soon as we set foot on the property. Now as long as whoever runs this place isn't trying to orchestrate a scheme to scare us off and renegotiate a mortgage, we should be in good shape.

But as we look around and wait for somebody to check us in, the lack of a presence becomes disconcerting. I lean over the counter and inspect the other side, where there are some notepads, travel brochures, and pieces of individually wrapped candy.

Nothing creepy or dirty or invasive, which is good, but nobody being here is a minus. The back area on the other side has an old computer, stacks of novels, and a bare wooden kitchen table.

"Maybe we should go right in and find out where we're supposed to stay on our own," I say, though Miles doesn't look keen on that.

"Somebody must be around. Who is the host supposed to be?" Taylor asks, dropping her bag and flopping in one of the wicker chairs.

"Her name is Margaret," Miles says, pulling out his phone to check, "and from the picture she looks like she uses a wheelchair or scooter. Oh, wait! She sent a message right around noon saying that she doesn't do well with the midday heat and has a pool in the back-yard where she spends most of the day. Evidently there are stairs behind the counter and to the left that will lead us to the second floor, which is all ours, and we can come and go as we please."

I blink, wishing Miles had noticed the message a little earlier before we spent time calling and waiting around in vain.

But after the flight and canvassing the island with varying degrees of effort, we're all ready to get into a comfortable living space to relax. The stairs aren't too difficult to find, and they lead up to a living room with four bedrooms and a bathroom set around the edges.

Although not as heavily furnished as the cabin in Hochatown, there are a couple of couches and a coffee table, brown-carpeted floor, cream-colored walls with paintings of sea birds, and a large-screen TV. A glance out the window tells me that the view is mostly of other buildings, but the sky is nice enough.

Hard not to feel underwhelmed after the resorts I saw, but it's still better than my apartment in Dallas by a mile.

"Kind of strange for the host not to show up so we can meet them, isn't it?" Wesley asks.

I take a deep breath and exhale. "It's probably for the best," I say. If Margaret had any idea what went on at our last Airbnb, she'd want to stay as far away from us as possible.

While Taylor reclines on a couch and Wesley heads into the bathroom, I peek into the different bedrooms, noticing that they all have twin beds. What?

Jerking my head while Miles is looking in a cabinet with DVDs, I gaze at him surreptitiously with a sudden ache in my chest. Granted, I hadn't shouted from the rooftops that we'd be sleeping together, but I hadn't been asked and would be happy to see how it goes.

But had he intentionally chosen all twin beds, or was this Airbnb all that was available? Of course, I'm sure we could make a twin bed rock if our hearts are really set on it, but it raises the question of if Miles isn't actually that interested in me or if he is feeling put upon by this whole trip.

The kiss we shared suddenly feels like a long time ago, and I wonder if I haven't been giving strong enough signals that I'm open to seeing what we might have. It's very possible all my spicy thoughts have not been translating to enough concrete hints. Or perhaps he's really conservative, inexperienced, or playing it safe, and I need to force the issue if we're ever going to get anywhere.

Sighing, I see Miles doesn't seem that impressed by the accommodations, though he's not complaining about it. His neutral face looks apathetic, and he appears tired, either from the flight or how much I'm asking him to do for me.

I know what to do.

"Alright, I do have some good news," I say as Wesley lumbers out of the bathroom, scratching himself shamelessly. "I was roaming around near The Ritz-Carlton when I saw a couple strolling in from a ways off down the beach. It was my parents, and that's where they're staying!"

The flash of excitement in Miles's eyes makes it all worth it, and Taylor and Wesley get caught up in it as well.

"Phew, that's a relief," Taylor says. "I was sure this whole trip was going to be an epic waste of time."

Miles comes right up to me and gives me a one-armed hug in congratulations.

"I honestly can't believe we've found them when they could've gone anywhere," he says.

It does feel like hitting the lottery, and we share some eye contact and glowing smiles.

"Two heads are better than one," I say but need to glance away when I notice Wesley heading straight for the stairs. "Hey, where are you going?"

He sheepishly looks over his shoulder.

"Uhh, I was going back out to the beach. If we've found them, we're done here, right? That was a lot of work for me, and I'm ready to kick back. For what it's worth, the champagne on the plane isn't that good."

"Wesley, I don't think so. Get back over here. You'll have time at the beach, but this isn't over yet," I say.

"Why not?" Taylor asks, lounging on the dated couch. "Now that you know where your parents are, you can just call the cops on them or whatever and have this wrapped up with a bow."

"Because that wouldn't get my sister out of prison. I need to catch them and make them help overturn her sentence. The only way to do that is to get some leverage on them," I explain, but Miles squints at me.

"And how do you expect to do that? The only way they'd be able to prove she didn't commit a crime would be if they admitted to it, right? They don't strike me as the type to take responsibility for their actions," he says, and I can hear the disdain in his voice.

If I didn't know better, I'd think Miles dislikes my parents almost as much as I do. Maybe it's the massive fraud scheme and egregious deceit.

A sneaky grin widens at the anticipation I feel.

"Leave that to me. Finding my parents isn't the only thing I did this morning. Unlike you jobless louts, I'm now gainfully employed at The Ritz-Carlton. All I had to do is tell them that I was willing to work for free for experience."

Wesley narrows his eyes at me.

"Uhh, it's not really gainful if you're not getting anything out of it, is it?"

"Not true!" I say, holding up a finger at him. "What I'm getting is access to my parents' room. While I'm pretending to clean, I'll be able to go through everything they have with them. There's no doubt in my mind that I'll be able to find something about their current identities, their connection to Bedrock, their future plans, or perhaps even something directly related to Melanie that would get her out of prison."

Taylor raises her eyebrows, and for once she doesn't seem to have any kind of a counterargument. Satisfied, I cross my arms. This is looking like I'm on the verge of checkmate, and all I have to do is make one last move.

The sensation I have of feeling pretty good about myself and my own cunning scheme doesn't last long, when I notice Miles becoming more contemplative and uncomfortable. My lips part, and a sinking feeling hits my gut even before he opens his mouth.

"It's not that simple," he says somberly, and his attempt to be gentle about it might be the scariest thing of all.

"What?" I ask, not sure if I want to know the answer.

He shakes his head and appears to have a hard time looking at me.

"The money, Emily. Unless they've got all the money they stole hoarded in their hotel room, this isn't going to help us get it back!"

Shutting my eyes to try to block out the sting, I chide myself.

Right, the money.

13

I don't want to believe that having free and clear access to all of my parents' belongings won't also enable us to get the money back.

"But, Miles," I say, sounding too much like I'm pleading, "maybe they have some papers about where their money is, or once they're forced to help Melanie, the authorities can take it back from them."

It all sounds reasonable to me, but Miles keeps shaking his head.

"That's not how it works here," he says. "They came to the Cayman Islands for a reason, remember? This is where money disappears. Untraceable transactions, no paper trail, and unless the United States authorities suddenly decide to use literal torture, there's no way they can force the location of the stolen money out of them. It may be gone for good. There's a good chance your parents may not even know exactly where it is."

Wincing, I feel like all of my good news isn't nearly as good now that the stolen money is still out of reach. I want to keep arguing with Miles that I'm right, but I have to accept he knows way more than me, then I can move on to dealing with it.

"So you're saying that they have to not only help get Melanie out of prison but also help us get the money back? They're never going to do that!" I shout bitterly.

Miles still has that look on his face like he's afraid to keep giving me bad news, like I'm going to either shatter into pieces or rip his head off. I feel like doing both at the same time.

"That's why it's so important to keep them and the money from getting out of the country," he says.

I glance around glumly at Wesley and Taylor's long faces, trying to buy time to figure out what we can do.

Taylor shakes her head sadly at me.

"Maybe you should take what you can, get your sister back, and call it a day. Let the authorities try their luck," she says, which sounds a lot to me like accepting failure. And it puts a look of dismay on Miles's face that I know he won't be able to tolerate.

"No, we're not giving up this easily. There has to be a way. Yes, I want my sister out of jail, but I'm not about to let my parents keep all of that dirty money in the process."

Suddenly, Wesley hops off the couch and raises his hand, signaling for attention. I don't want to give it to him but have no choice, and he knows it.

"Hold on, everybody," he says with a big grin to go along with his big chin. "We're blowing this problem way out of proportion. There's an easy solution here."

He waits for someone to respond, but nobody does. I scoff, Taylor rolls her eyes, and Miles simply watches him.

"Don't you—"

"No, we're not going to ask. Just tell us," I say.

Wesley lowers his eyes at me and seems to wrestle with qualms about going on after nobody said the magic word for him. Eventually, his vanity wins out, and he has to keep talking before we start to ignore him.

"We know where they're staying, and we have access to their room. Why don't we go in, happen to be in there when they come back, and urge them strongly to hand over the money and cooperate with Emily's little felon sister."

Not liking how he referred to Melanie, I glower at him, but Miles astutely picks up on the bigger problem. "Urge them strongly?"

"Heh," Wesley says, getting a kick out of his own euphemism. "I'm not saying we do anything bad. All we need to do is tell them we'll do things to them if they don't do what we want. Then when they comply, we don't have to do them. It only takes being convincing enough that they don't call our bluff."

"I think that's called a threat. You want us to threaten them," Taylor says, cringing.

Wesley shakes his head.

"'Threat' has such a negative connotation though. This is more like peer pressure without them being our peers. Considering what they did to get the money, this is nothing," he argues.

Miles shoots me a quick look that makes it clear his disapproval goes without saying. I release an exasperated breath, not dismissing Wesley's criminal idea as quickly as I'd like, but we do have to do something, and my preference would be for it not to involve threatening to hurt anyone.

"I appreciate the idea, but we can't do that to them, even after what they've done. I will say this though. My parents being who they are—and at some level needing their cooperation to get what we want from them—means there's going to have to be deception involved. The question is how much we can live with," I say.

My mind is already working, but nothing comes quickly to mind, and there are no immediate answers from anyone else.

"I suppose asking them to do the right thing wouldn't work," Miles says, and I regretfully shake my head.

"They don't think like that," I say.

I catch eyes with Taylor on the couch, looking eager to help yet clueless about what we could do. She puts her hands up, and I nod, appreciating that she's trying and being attentive instead of attempting to stab me in the back.

The window beckons, and I look out at the blue sky and the wispy clouds floating far overhead. My mind drifts back to seeing my parents at the beach, carefree and happy. I really can't see any of us tying my parents to a chair and threatening their lives, but a trick might be more our style.

But what?

Glancing back, I see that Miles has gotten himself a glass of water. Wesley is giving Taylor a back rub as she leans forward onto her legs. I imagine my sister in a dreary prison, watching her twenties wrongfully slip away. The job I got at The Ritz-Carlton is still promising, but it's not going to be enough.

An idea strikes me, one that starts small at first but keeps growing until it seems so big I might burst.

When I turn away from the window and rejoin the group, they notice that something is up.

"I've got it," I say. "There's a way we can get them to give the money back. It is a trick, but we don't have to threaten them or push them to do anything they won't already want to do."

"What is it?" Miles asks, and I cast him a sidelong smirk.

"I wasn't going to make you ask."

"I know, but I wanted to anyway."

Amused, it takes me a second to get back on to my train of thought. This is already feeling so promising.

"My parents have just gotten here, as did their stolen money. They're not going to be staying at The Ritz forever, and their money is probably in a temporary place too. Why don't we convince them to give it to us?"

Taylor crosses her arms, and I'm ready for her to try to pick apart my plan.

"But how can we do that?" she asks.

"We tell them we have the best place to put their money. It's just like what we did at Bedrock. We pitch an investment plan in a special Cayman Islands bank that will both keep their money hidden and give them a bonanza in the form of interest and investment returns!" I say.

I glance at Miles and can see he's skeptical about the idea because of the dishonesty, but he's not dismissing it outright, at least for my sake.

"You want to con them out of the money they conned," Wesley says admiringly, but I wince, afraid it'll turn Miles off.

"There are three parts. We open up our own Cayman Islands hidden account at any bank, we get the message to my parents that there's this amazing bank on the island that's the perfect shelter with amazing perks, and then they come to us to open up their own account and transfer the money into our one account, which they think is theirs."

With a sharp clap of his hands, Wesley steps closer with a broad smile. At least I've sold one of them on my scheme. It may not be a genius-level plan, but it might be good enough to work.

"And step four is that we split the money evenly, twenty-five percent each," he says, his eyes glazing over as he seemingly has already started counting his money.

I open my mouth, but Miles beats me to it. "No, then we'd be able to hand all the money over to the authorities to return to the robbed investors."

Wesley, a few inches taller than Miles, leers at him skeptically.

"But surely we could keep ten percent and split that," he says.

"No."

"A couple of million each, then. We'd be working hard, and this would be way more than anyone would get back otherwise."

Miles groans. "All of the stolen money has to go back immediately. In fact, we'd want to contact the investigators in the states the second the transfer is initiated."

I nod feverishly, getting the impression that Miles is talking himself into it. Does Wesley know he is baiting Miles into being involved if he can spell out his own terms? If so, I won't begrudge Wesley the airplane champagne any longer.

"We're in agreement, then," I say. It looks like we're all smiling brightly, until I notice that one of us isn't and turn to Taylor, who looks like she might have some bad indigestion. "OK, Taylor, why won't this work?"

She crosses her arms and leans back on the couch.

"And how do you think we're supposed to do all that? Don't you think your parents will recognize you, even if you're now a brunette? And they'll spot the rest of us if we both try to pitch them on a bank and then also are there pretending like we work for it. I don't see how we pull this off."

She raises her hands, like it's the most obvious thing in the world. I open my mouth, ready to shoot it all down and brush it off, but I get stuck when I realize she has a point and there's no easy counterargument. Shaking my head, I try to tease out a little more of my stroke of genius as fast as I can.

"Of course we wouldn't be able to have anybody do multiple parts. Even if I can't speak to them directly and am focused on getting into their room, you and Wesley can still split dealing with them. It's like this. Taylor pitches them on the bank, and Wes gets them to transfer the money into our account."

I don't see the problem until I catch Miles's horrified look. His wide eyes say it all. Are we really going to trust Wesley to handle routing the money? Before either of us can voice the problem, Taylor scoffs.

"What, am I supposed to just walk up to your parents and tell them I know a place they can park all the money they fled the States with?"

The underwhelming feeling in my gut comes on strong, and I knee-jerk react in the best way I can.

"OK, Wesley pitches the bank, and Taylor acts like the bank employee," I suggest, hopeful.

"Perfect. I've got this," Wesley says confidently, and I have vivid memories of all of his sleazy scam pitches. My parents will see that a mile away.

"Actually—"

"So now you want me to be a retail bank representative?" Taylor interrupts derisively. "I can't answer any questions about investments or how a bank works. I was in accounting, not financial planning."

Wincing, I scramble to come up with another alternative before it starts to seem like my brilliant idea isn't going to work. I blurt out the first thing that comes to my mind.

"Fine. Both you and Wesley need to find my parents. Don't even talk to them at all. Act like you're a young couple who got a big windfall and is trying to hide it from the US government. Slip in our bank's name and what a great opportunity it is. They'll hear you and come find us on their own."

Taylor opens her mouth to shred my idea again, but nothing comes out, and she looks to Wesley, who has a coy grin. They both nod at each other slowly, and for a second I think I'm in the clear.

"We can do that," she says, "but then who's going to sell them on a fake bank and investment scheme that suckers all of their money out of them?"

With those two being assigned the part of dangling the bait, that only leaves me and Miles to run the actual scheme. And with me being too close to them to pose as an employee for a bank that doesn't exist peddling a bank account that's actually ours, that only leaves one of us.

And that one of us is known for having a strong boundary between right and wrong and likes to only stay on the right side of it.

As the answer dawns on us, Taylor, Wesley, and I slowly turn to Miles, who stands there bug-eyed and speechless.

I smile painfully at him, surely coming off more desperate than cute.

Getting the stolen money back isn't really going to depend on Miles lying, is it?

14

The uncomfortable moment drags on, Miles looking repulsed enough that it seems he's on the verge of being ill. I try to tell myself it wouldn't be such a big deal. He'd just be conducting the very same type of scam that my parents did, except on only one very deserving target.

But to Miles I know it's a very big deal. He loathes these types of things, and the thought of participating in something like it has to be gut-wrenching. I'm honestly shocked he didn't straight out say no.

Are my doe eyes working?

Wesley and Taylor have the good sense to keep their mouths shut while Miles and I feel each other out. I'm looking at him plaintively, lips slightly parted and clasping a finger in front of my hips. This is the pose for quiet desperation.

I can't help thinking that his decision is really going to hinge on how he feels about me and the way I look, and I mentally cycle through my list of physical flaws.

Eyes never leaving me, Miles begins working his mouth and swallowing, like he's chewing on something tough. A breath, and he appears calm but worn down.

"I don't have a better idea," he mutters, not exactly a ringing endorsement.

I clap my hands, lighting up. "Great! It won't be as bad as you think. Trust me," I say, having no choice but to forge ahead and hope that my optimism will make the situation more palatable.

And despite Miles's misgivings, he dives into the work of preparing to carry out our plan, which turns out to rest largely on his shoulders as well. I write some text that I think will appeal to my parents, but he's the one who has the laptop and needs to put together an entire website.

Fortunately he has code from another project he's done that he can largely recycle, but getting things ready still burns up the entire afternoon and beyond.

Wesley and Taylor help for a little while, particularly with converting the front entrance of our rental into something that might pass for a bank branch's front office, but before long they announce they need some space to rehearse their pitch to my parents.

Clearly what they really meant was that they were going out for fun, which didn't seem like a bad idea.

Except Miles and I have more work to do.

I'm sitting at the kitchen table, typing on his laptop to create some flyers we can print and pass off as bank promotional material, but I keep getting distracted as Miles creates a sign for the front door with some pieces of lumber and paint I found by the trash left over from a renovation or something.

He's working hard, some sweat forming along the hairline on the back of his neck, and I start thinking he'd be a lot more comfortable if he took his shirt off. I wouldn't mind it...

A last glance at the screen confirms my gut instinct that I'm far too distracted to write one more word, not when there are other crucial aspects of this operation that haven't received enough attention, namely the situation between Miles and me.

The shape of his profile and the way he's working with his hands strike me as very masculine, and it calls to mind something I was thinking about before. I've been so focused on finding my parents that I haven't made enough time for having fun or being affectionate.

Getting up, I wonder if we can cover both of those bases at once.

Are we ready to dupe the crooks? No. Is what we have done so far passable enough? Only time will tell. But either way, doing something to get Miles's heart into it a little more will help.

I walk over feeling oddly self-conscious approaching him, because this is not the way I usually do this. My MO has always been to keep my heart hidden, be the one who's less attached, and play hard to get. And even when a relationship starts to heat up, I still play hard to get on repeat until it fizzles out.

Maybe it's because I've reached the ripe old age of twenty-four, but I'm starting to feel ready to be caught, if it's a man I can respect and admire.

But instead of straight up coming on to me, Miles has instead listened to me, taken up my cause, and put in back-breaking work to help me.

How am I supposed to play it cool when I'm so indebted to him and still have to make the first move?

He pulls the brush away and then peels off a piece of tape, revealing a perfectly painted sign reading Greater Cayman Bank, the name we landed on that would have the same initials and plausibly have the same transfer code as Grand Cayman Bank.

Miles rises from his crouched position and breathes a sigh of relief, looking over his work.

"I'm glad I didn't screw that up," he says.

I smirk, thinking, *I hope I'll be saying the same thing a little while from now.*

Setting a finger on his shoulder, I draw his attention away from the sign and back where it belongs, on me.

"We've put in enough work, don't you think? Let's head out and have some fun. Find a beach or dinner somewhere?"

His eyebrows rise at the suggestion, getting my hopes up, but then something seems to weigh on him.

"That does sound nice, but I'm actually kind of tired and would rather hang out," he says.

Nodding, I eagerly read into that and think it actually sounds better than any of my suggestions.

"Come to think of it, I'm feeling the same way. And we've spent enough time in the living room. Maybe we should try one of the bedrooms. Yours or mine?"

He squints at me and then rubs his eyes, which are a little red.

"Why would I sleep in your bedroom? It's already been a long day with the flight and everything," he says.

Oh, he's actually tired and not simply saying that as an excuse so that we can stay in and feel each other up. He should get used to going on almost no sleep like I do. Burying my disappointment, I buck up and attempt to persevere.

"Your room it is. And I have an idea. You don't know this about me, but I've been training as a massage therapist. Why don't you let me try out my skills and we can see where that goes?"

Miles narrows his eyes at me suspiciously.

"When did you start doing that?"

"Right now?" I say quickly with a cheesy grin.

Miles blinks, his faint smile carrying way too much ambivalence for what I've thrown out there. If this were any other guy, our pants would already be off, but the whole reason I'm interested is because he's not like other guys. He's different, and it's forcing me to work harder at this than I've ever needed to.

Sighing, Miles says, "Can I take a rain check on that? I'm so wiped out that if I don't rest up, I'll be completely nonfunctional when this goes down."

Clenching my jaw in frustration, I try my best to react and adapt to what Miles needs right now.

"Then let me at least say thank you for everything you've been doing. I know this is asking a lot, and none of it is easy for you, but it really means so much to me."

I wrap my arms around him and give him a brief squeeze, feeling his hands rest on my back. A kiss on the cheek, all innocent and sweet, is my attempt to meet what he might appreciate in this moment, and then we say goodnight.

Although we're headed to bed early with a big day tomorrow starting with my new "job," I watch Miles slip into his room alone and wonder how I'm supposed to sleep feeling so sexually frustrated and unsatisfied.

It looks like the most exciting part of my evening is going to be a cold shower.

15

It doesn't take me more than a few minutes working at The Ritz-Carlton to realize that the only reason anybody works any job is because they get paid for it.

I also quickly discover that the girl with the long blond hair and the nose stud who was so nice when I seemed like a resort guest is not nearly as nice when I'm a new resort employee.

But it turns out Sadie is in charge of me, and as she scrutinizes me in the company's cleaning staff uniform, tan with gold stripes, I get the sense that she'd rather not be if she had the choice.

"It's not too difficult, and you're going to learn on the job, following the rest of the housekeeping staff. You'll start outside in the morning by raking the beach for any garbage or other debris that drifted in. You work your way in to the pool area, disinfecting and scrubbing chairs, tables, or other surfaces. Open all the umbrellas, mop the deck, vacuum the walkways, and stay out of the way of any guests," she explains as if she's given this spiel a thousand times.

"Got it," I say, thinking how I probably won't be doing very much of any of that.

Sadie, raising eyebrows that are darker than her hair, looks at me warily. When I nod to try to convey that I've heard her loud and clear, she shakes her head dismissively.

"Late morning, the cleaning staff does the interior hallways, common spaces, and conference rooms that are unoccupied. There's a short break for lunch, and then in the afternoon the guest rooms are cleaned between check-out and check-in times. Again, you'll be training under a more senior staff member, so do what they do. It's not that hard," she says, a lilt in her voice that makes it clear she wouldn't clean a guest room if her life depended on it.

My life does depend on it, unfortunately, as does my sister's. Sadie continues to explain the fine art of scrubbing hotel bathrooms and changing sheets, but I've already gotten as far as I need with the instructions and start to tune her out. Once I make it to the afternoon, all I really need to do is find out which room is my parents' and then get into it to find something incriminating I can use to make them help my sister.

There are so many possibilities. Simply getting their current fake IDs and threatening to hand them over to the US or Cayman Islands authorities would scare them. The plane tickets from Dallas would connect them to their escape. Maybe there is some communication with their fake FBI agents, connecting them to a bigger criminal network.

There's no telling what they might be up to that I could use.

"Did you get all that?" Sadie asks, and I blink hard, realizing she's still talking at me.

"Of course," I say with a relaxed smile.

"Do you need me to say that again?" She takes a big breath, like she's about to repeat everything she said verbatim.

"No," I say, waving my hands. "I got every word of it. You don't have to worry about a thing."

The way her glassy blue eyes glare gives me a window into

the battle raging inside of her between wanting to be condescending and not caring at all about me. It makes it hard to believe how friendly she was when I walked up to the desk to ask her about my parents.

"To be clear," Sadie says, lowering her eyes at me, "if you happen to see your friends, you're not allowed to interact with them at all. Even if you're volunteering for experience, you're here to work, not socialize."

A short, sharp chuckle escapes my mouth before I can hold it back, making her flinch.

"Oh, you don't have to worry about that. I don't have any friends here," I say, staring at her intently.

Her mouth drops open a bit as she grasps my message, and the next thing I know she's turned tail and starts marching back to the desk.

That leaves me free to begin my unpaid labor, which as per Sadie's instructions takes me outside to the seashore in the cool, early morning atmosphere with a light breeze drifting in off the surf.

There are a few others on the cleaning staff with me, and we head out with trash bags and extension claws to pick up any garbage. I'm so busy staring at the clouds and the distant horizon that I barely realize what's around me.

After all, I was just here yesterday, and the beach was completely clean, so I figure this task is really more of an excuse to walk up and down the shoreline for a while.

But, oh no. Once I'm a dozen paces beyond The Ritz's pools, I see what the tide brought in, and the entire stretch of beach now looks like a dump. At first I stare, gobsmacked, and I only get more grossed out from there.

Various items—plastic bags, bottles, toy pieces, other bits of garbage, even a couple of used diapers that floated in from wherever—litter the beach like little invaders trying to destroy the beauty of the beach and the resort.

Considering I have time to kill before Wesley and Taylor show up to hunt down my parents, I do something I vow not to make a habit of. I focus my attention on what I'm supposed to be doing and get to work.

Disgusted the entire time, I clear the beach until my bag is almost too heavy to carry. The constant motion is making my shoulder sore too, but no one else is complaining about anything. Every so often I sneak a look at the brilliant horizon and the rising sun, but mostly I buckle down and snap up as much of the refuse as I can.

By the time my second bag is almost full, it's not so early in the morning, and some of the guests are starting to appear on balconies and through windows, likely looking for breakfast before spending more time outdoors.

We shift our attention to the pool area—cleaning up, sweeping, mopping, vacuuming, and wiping surfaces—but I'm much less motivated to do things for other people as I was when I felt like I was doing something for the beach.

The morning ticks on, and I start to wonder if I need to find a way inside to see if Wesley and Taylor have found my parents while they're having breakfast or something.

We never went over in detail exactly what they would say other than our fake bank's name, and I know I'll have doubts that they'll be able to convince my parents to act on the bait until I can see for myself they've done it.

And there are all the ways they could blow it, like contradicting themselves or acting nervous.

It's not that I don't trust Wesley and Taylor... OK, it is that I don't trust them.

"Things look pretty good out here. I'll get started inside," I say to a stick-thin lady with frizzy black hair who is training me.

I start walking toward the double doors to head inside when I see a couple of people coming out at the same time. It's a woman with wingtips and a button nose next to her suave husband with the salt-and-pepper hair and emerging tan.

My parents are heading outside, and they're coming right at me, only bare glass doors between us.

16

I nearly roll my ankle as I twist hard and start scampering out of the way, breaking into a hobble and hustling out of their line of sight. The closest place to hide is the vacant cabana, which won't be opening until the afternoon, and I practically dive into it to make sure they don't see me.

The last thing I need is to screw everything up by letting them know I'm here.

On my knees with a rag in hand, I slowly rise enough to peer over the counter while pretending to scrub the interior side of the bar. Even if they look in my direction, all they'll see is my dark hair, which should give me some cover as long as they don't look at me too closely.

Diedre and Marty Marks stroll out onto the deck like they own the place and survey the pools and waterfront, no doubt appreciating the pristine state of the beach, which I spent hours of grueling work cleaning.

It dawns on me that I'm holding my breath watching them, noticing Dad's colorful Hawaiian shirt and Mom's bikini bottom under a cotton t-shirt, her fingernails and toenails in matching bright-pink polish.

The last time I saw them was back in the Bedrock executive suite, which was only a few days ago but feels like a past life. Without their fancy clothes and rich trappings, they look like regular tourists ready to relax, not merciless predators who've robbed people of millions and cost hundreds of people their jobs.

Smiling shyly, Mom looks like a love-struck teenager when she glances at Dad, who takes off his sunglasses to kiss her without risking an uncomfortable collision. Although the kiss isn't long, she sets her hand on his upper back while he brushes his fingers over her hip.

My breathing becomes more like a wheeze as I watch them express how much they love each other and no one else.

Shaking my head slowly and keeping out of sight as much as possible, I wait for them to continue on down the beach, perhaps giving me time to find Wesley and Taylor and get them in good position for when they return.

But they forgo the beach, even passing up the chairs lined up closer to the water, and decide to park themselves in the chairs closest to the deck, which happen to be barely ten paces from the cabana.

My anxiety kicks up as they get closer and make themselves comfortable, producing a bottle of sunblock and setting a phone on a small table between their chairs. If they're here and planning to stay a while, this is perfect, except for how they're basically trapping me inside the cabana with the thatched roof, liquor bottles, and glasses glistening in the morning sun.

Without a phone of my own, there's no way for me to contact anybody from here. I do get some looks from the other cleaning staff as well, spurring me to keep up my ruse that I'm here to work, but inside I'm screaming that this is our chance.

The temptation hits me to try to hop the back side of the counter so I can skitter away without them seeing me. Their backs are to me, so as long as I don't knock over a glass or flop on the deck, I should be able to get away.

As I'm about to execute my daring maneuver, the nearest interior doors swing open, and out walk Wesley and Taylor in swimsuits. I'm so relieved my knees nearly buckle.

There are probably one hundred beach chairs on the ocean-side of The Ritz-Carlton, 95 percent of them unoccupied, and Wesley and Taylor happen to pick the ones right next to the Markses.

I stare at them to make sure everything is going right until Taylor happens to glance my way and recognize me. She's all business, and her look warns me to pay attention to what I'm doing so that my presence doesn't spoil this. It's enough to make me start scrubbing the bar in earnest, not even looking at them directly most of the time.

The next time I look up, they're sprawled out on the beach chairs next to my parents, all of them close enough to me that I could speak to them without raising my voice at all.

Once they're all there, I expect Wesley and Taylor to get started on their pitch, but instead silence reigns for at least ten minutes. After a while, I realize that sitting down and immediately talking up an investment scheme might be off-putting. Still, I'm impatient and want to get this over with.

I'm tempted again to try to reach out and nudge them in some way, but they don't look back at me once. Also probably for the best, because my parents might notice.

"How much longer are we going to be staying here, Chett?" Taylor asks, and I have to cover my mouth to hold in the laughter.

I didn't know we were going to be resurrecting Chett for this. Didn't he die in Hochatown too?

Wesley leans back and puts his hands behind his head. He's

seated right next to my dad on his left, but he doesn't so much as glance in their direction.

"We can stay as long as we like. There's no rush," he says, so comfortable that he yawns.

Taylor leans his way. I can't see their faces, only her ponytail swaying as she replies, "It's expensive here though, isn't it?"

Nodding, I scrub the same section of the bar that I've been cleaning for the past five minutes, smiling to myself as I start to see the direction they're going. It's early, but it just might work. My parents barely seem to notice the couple directly next to them, but I know they're not deaf.

Wesley shrugs. "What does it matter? We could get a room at every resort on the island if we want. Ever since I hit it big with the—"

"Chett!" Taylor interrupts. "Shouldn't you keep it down? You know there will be consequences if anyone finds out."

The frustrated sigh that Wesley produces sounds a little too authentic.

"For the twentieth time, relax," he says at full volume. "That's why everybody comes here. You think I'm the only one who figured out how to get rich the easy way?"

Crossing her arms, Taylor grumps at him, and I can picture her pouty lips and furrowed brows perfectly in my mind after seeing them directed at me so many times.

"You weren't like this yesterday," she mutters, and now I do have to strain to hear.

"It's not a big deal."

"Tell me," Taylor insists, and Wesley glances at her.

"It's too complicated for you," he snaps, and Taylor gives him a hard glare.

Either their acting has gotten really good, or they're veering off script a little in a way that's pissing her off. Wesley seems to be enjoying goading her, and I catch a glimpse of his devilish smirk.

"I know it's a lot of money, but what's made you so comfortable with it all of a sudden?" she asks, sounding like more of a demand than I'd like.

I'm surprised her tone doesn't make my parents look over, but they're still surely completely aware of everything.

"Alright, I'll tell you," he says, still teasing her.

Taylor leans away and puts her hand on her face.

"No, now I don't want to know."

That draws Wesley's attention, and all I can do is grit my teeth.

"Yes, you do."

"Not really. You can keep your secret. What do I care?" she says.

"It's not that big a deal. I found a good place to park the bundle where it can do some extra work for us," he explains tersely. "The interest rates are amazing, there are special perks, and best of all, no questions from anybody."

Taylor watches him carefully for a moment.

"I thought we already had the money in a good bank."

Wesley shakes his head.

"Nobody keeps their money in the same bank that they transferred their funds into the country to. That's just asking for it to be found and reversed. You have to take the extra step to really hide it with a Cayman Islands domestic transfer. I found the perfect place for it. Greater Cayman Bank," he explains, and I smile and hope my parents caught that name.

"I've never heard of it," Taylor says.

Scoffing, Wesley mutters in the opposite direction, practically saying it right to my dad, "That's not surprising."

From the cabana, I can see Taylor's mouth pop open, aghast. I'm starting to get the impression something happened between them last night. The twin beds may not be working out for them any better than they are for me. If they tried to share one, maybe that's why they're bringing some crankiness into their performance.

"I understand this stuff better than you think. After all, I'm an acc... I'm good at math," she says, catching herself.

My heart skips a beat, wondering if she was about to say she was an accountant or, worse, had worked at Bedrock. I'm glad she hadn't crossed paths with either of my parents while they worked there. Those in the executive suite must not've visited the accounting department in person often.

"Thank goodness you have that going for you," Wesley says sarcastically, and my eyes widen.

"What's that supposed to mean?" Taylor shoots back, on the edge of her beach chair in his direction.

My scrubbing comes to a stop, and I'm staring openly at them now. Are they seriously getting into a fight in the middle of their pitch to my parents? It's obvious now that they had some kind of problem last night, but I had no idea because I had to leave for "work" so early.

That look from Taylor wasn't an all-business look. No, she's super pissed about something. And Wesley is dismissive and patronizing. I don't know whom to be angrier at. Can't they work this out later?

Wesley casts a cold glance at Taylor before rubbing his neck.

"If I have to spell it out for you, it means there are some other things you're not so good at," he says.

Taylor gasps and clenches her fists. For a second, I think she's going to reach out and slug him. I wouldn't blame her, having done it myself recently.

"I haven't heard you complain before. Like, what wasn't good?"

My stomach turns as Wesley chuckles awkwardly, and I pray

we don't get the actual answer. I have to imagine whatever banking advice my parents heard is getting overshadowed now that we've moved on to salacious mudslinging.

"All I'm saying is I've had better."

I can see Taylor turning red from here, and she looks like she's about to explode. The thought hits me to run over there and yell at them to abort, as if it could get any worse. If I'm the director, can I say "cut" and end this scene?

"You want someone else?" Taylor growls.

"I didn't say that."

"No, but you meant it. We shouldn't have come here."

"Too late for that," Wesley mutters.

My parents are doing a good job minding their own business, but I'm sure they're laughing hysterically to themselves. Meanwhile all I can do is fume and cry that these two can't keep their act together for five minutes.

"Then who is it? Who was so good that you've gotten tired of me?"

I squint, focusing in on Wesley, trying to figure out where this is going.

"No," he says, shaking his head.

"Tell me!" Taylor insists, reaching and grabbing his sleeve.

Wesley looks down at her grip on him and clenches his jaw. The simmering anger on his face is something I've never seen before. He's often clueless and manipulative and completely without any sense of ethics, but getting mad has never been his style.

"I don't—"

"You'd just lie to me anyway. I shouldn't have trusted you. Can't even come out with it when you want to dump me for someone else. Who is it?"

Jerking hard, Wesley tears his sleeve away from Taylor, who

is gritting her teeth at him. He tries to get up, but she clutches his arm and holds him back, causing him to snap at her.

"Emily!"

I nearly collapse against the cabana counter, stricken and speechless. My parents both turn their heads, and I feel like I'm going to be sick. So much for getting my sister out of prison.

Didn't I say that everything Wesley touches turns into a disaster?

17

"What?" Taylor gasps, clear-eyed and shaken out of her frenzy once Wesley says my name.

My skin crawls as I realize that Wesley is admitting to being interested in me and prefers me to Taylor. Being with him all those years ago was a mistake, and so was considering letting him back into my life during our girls' trip. Yet somehow he did weasel back into my life and is wreaking the same kind of havoc he did when I was eighteen.

I can see the look on my parents' faces, now fully turned to the two of them, and I can see the damage is so profound that even Wesley has the sense to be reticent about it, growing pale and skittish.

"Who are you talking about?" my mother asks, and with her head turned I can see the diamonds in her earrings, surely the ones she took from her office when she thought I was lying dead on the floor.

Wesley, mouth agape, gives my mother a terrified stare, seeming to know he crossed the line. Taylor rushes to fill the silence.

"You said my name. What?" she says. "Are you going to tell me who you want or not?"

"Uhh, nobody. I was just... There's nobody else. I'm sorry. I was annoyed about last night. I'll forget about it," Wesley says while my parents eye them carefully.

"My daughter's name is Emily," Mom says, somewhere between a casual comment and an accusation.

Taylor cracks a grin and waves it off, an amazing feat in light of what happened.

"It's a common girls' name. You made a good choice. It's too bad having it myself means I can't use it too. 'Emily Jr.' seems a bit much, not that I'm going to need to pick baby names anytime soon," Taylor says, glaring daggers at Wesley.

Her repartee is better than she probably could've expected. Diedre appears thrown off at being complimented about me, shaking her head and turning to Dad, who shrugs and reaches out to spontaneously massage her shoulder.

Still unsettled, I breathe a cautious sigh of relief, hoping Taylor has managed to salvage the situation after Wesley started talking with his reproductive system instead of his central nervous system. Whether my parents will remember anything about Greater Cayman Bank remains to be seen, but at least I haven't been outed for being involved.

I still have to wonder though why this conversation got so far off track in the first place. Neither Wesley nor Taylor could stick to the script in the midst of whatever relationship blowup they're having, and it almost ruined our chance at getting the money back.

"I'm going back to the room," Wesley says, getting up before they can dig an even deeper hole.

"This isn't over!" Taylor gets up to follow him at a trot, and she doesn't know how right she is.

I break out of the cabana, stalking after them while turning away with a washrag held up to hide my face from my parents as much as possible. Wesley and Taylor are barely through the interior doors when I catch them, literally.

Grabbing both of them by the fabric over their shoulders, I steer them away from the front desk and down an adjacent hallway, this one leading to the shuffleboard court and sauna.

"Ack, Emily!" Wesley groans.

"Keep your voice down!" I shout.

"What a disaster," Taylor grumbles, and I jostle her shoulder enough to make her stumble.

"And what about you, almost spilling that you're an accountant and then needling him over and over?"

"It's not my fault," she whines, causing me to look at her face and see that her composure is slipping right off.

I let go as we get to an alcove with some white-painted columns and plenty of visibility down the two ends of the empty hallway to see if anyone else is coming. Standing there, I can see Taylor is starting to tear up, bearing the brunt of Wesley's confession that my parents couldn't understand.

Wesley has a mopey look on his face, glancing at me occasionally in what I can only imagine are fleeting attempts to gauge my interest.

"You had one job! What happened that you two couldn't get through one conversation without bringing your own mess into it?" I ask through my teeth.

I'm breathing heavily, nearly shaking with how upset I feel. It doesn't help when Wesley shrugs.

"It's not your business," he mutters, setting me off.

"What?" I say, waving my arms. "If you two can fork while I'm asleep three feet away, and bring me up with my parents right next to you, it sounds a lot like my business!"

Taylor scowls and then points at Wesley.

"You tell her."

Wesley rolls his eyes and shrugs.

"We were out with a great crowd, and I didn't want to leave them," he says. "It's not a big deal. Not everyone has to do it every day."

I can barely blink before Taylor starts blurting out, "That is such a joke. A great crowd? You were avoiding me! I knew it meant something then, and you admitted as much outside."

"No, it doesn't," he said, but she shakes her head.

"There's no use lying," Taylor insists, turning to me. "You must know what he's like."

I flinch at the reminder that I was with him and should know something about his habits, but as much as I've tried to forget, it's hard not to feel like she has a point. But what they did or didn't do last night isn't the problem.

Scowling, I turn away with my eyelids fluttering shut, trying to figure out how to say this in a way that would be fair, before turning to Wesley.

"Hey, listen to me carefully. I'm not the same person I was when we were together. We've talked about this, and I don't want to live like that or be like that. Things keep happening that make you say you want to be more responsible and stop taking advantage of other people, but then you try to take things from Miles's apartment or get him charged for drinks when he's already paying for everything."

I'm trying to be honest and non-argumentative, but Wesley can't meet my eyes, and his body language is closed off, which frustrates me.

He scoffs, "Miles isn't as great as you think. Imagine somebody who can't go into a hotel and look around without somebody holding his hand. I saw him at one of the resorts he was assigned. He barely went inside. He's socially inept, if you ask me."

That makes keeping civil more difficult, and I have to take a second to keep myself steady.

"This isn't about Miles, Wesley. Look at me. I'm not the right person for you, and you're not the right person for me. What you have with Taylor is between the two of you, but we are not going to be getting back together, ever. Don't hold out hope for it. I want to live in a way I can respect that doesn't take advantage of other people."

Wesley raises an eyebrow at me, nodding facetiously.

"So you're going to work another job that you lied to get into so you can access your parents' room and search their belongings without their consent."

I flinch, the friction feeling like it's grinding in my head.

"I didn't lie. I'm just not getting paid. Eventually, once I get through this, I won't have to do things like this anymore," I say, squirming.

Wesley shakes his head.

"Emily, you keep saying that, yet you keep doing things like this. The only person you're deceiving here is yourself, thinking that you're any different from us."

I'm about to say something when Taylor, teary-eyed and with a quivering lip, snorts at him and shakes her head.

"Sorry, in case you missed it, there is no 'us' anymore. And I don't have to get the same lesson over and over to learn it. I'm done with this stuff. When you're with someone who only wants to scam other people, I guess it's only a matter of time before you get scammed. Well, I've had enough. It's a good thing this place has four bedrooms, and as soon as we get back, I don't want to see you again," she says.

Her venting raises Wesley's hackles, and the last thing I want is for us to be unable to get through this together, but he looks aggrieved and defensive, his eyebrows furrowed and his upper lip raised like a dog about to bite.

I hold up my hands, ready to defuse the situation.

"Hey, it's alright. We can't—"

"Emily!" a voice calls harshly from down the hallway, and I jerk my head to see Sadie stalking toward me from the front desk area, her white-blond hair swaying lightly as she power-walks my way.

I naturally drift away from Wesley and Taylor, even though both of them still look ready to snap at each other. I have no choice but to hold my tongue.

"Yes?" I ask pleasantly as Sadie arrives and sets her hands on her narrow hips.

"Please let our guest services and concierge staff handle our guests. That way you can keep focused on your duties," she says with a disingenuously sweet tone.

"I'm so sorry, of course. They had a question, and I thought it would be rude to ignore them."

"She's right," Wesley says, and I breathe a sigh of relief, sure Sadie will have to back off now that I have the support of this pair masquerading as guests. "I was asking how much is best to tip the cleaning staff, and she said one hundred dollars a night is expected."

My eyes balloon as I shift slowly to Sadie, whose pale skin is turning red before my eyes.

Taylor quickly speaks up, "Don't listen to him. He's a big fibber. All we wanted was to know if we could get a couple of extra bathroom towels."

That makes Sadie hold her tongue, and I stand with her as Taylor takes Wesley by the wrist and leads him down the opposite hallway, neither of them looking back at us.

Once they're a ways down the hall, I shrug at Sadie, who does not look fully placated after Taylor's correction.

"I told you about talking to guests and don't want to see it again, no matter what it's about," she howls, making me wonder what kind of childhood she had to become so domineering. She should try a few years on the streets of Dallas.

"Right. I'm sorry," I say.

"Get back to work," she adds. "It's time to clean the rooms."

I smile, glad to be getting back on track and not at all feeling bad for deceiving Sadie about the reason I'm working here. I can't wait to find something in my parents' room that will help me and my sister.

"My pleasure."

18

Although ostensibly I'm supposed to be cleaning rooms, which doesn't sound nearly as appealing as cleaning the beach, I have a much more important task in mind.

I need to find out which room my parents are in.

And if I can do that while the two of them are cavorting around by the pools or ocean-side or having lunch somewhere, I should have plenty of time to perform a very thorough search for anything that might help my sister, my parents' countless victims, or myself.

But there's one notable problem. Sadie hates me and is guarding the front desk and the other reception staff. After what happened with Taylor and Wesley, Sadie will rip my head off if I come around asking about which room some guests are in.

That leaves me with an unclear path forward, especially considering I hardly know this place and have no idea who else might have that information. It's half tempting to head out and snoop around my parents to see if they're carrying a numbered room key or if they mention their room number.

Perhaps one of them will need to run back to the room for something, allowing me to follow.

But all of those possibilities put me at risk of being exposed and caught. I'll pass on giving my mother another chance to finish what she started in her office.

Roaming the hallways with my arms full of toilet paper, I try to get a sense of the rooms and quickly gather that ground-floor and first-floor rooms are pretty modest and are unlikely to be the ones that my parents picked.

But the two floors above them run end to end with the kind of palatial rooms the Markses would be partial to, and there are at least fifty of them.

"Can you help me with this?" one of the other cleaning staff members asks, and I assist her in making a bed while surreptitiously inspecting the personal belongings on the dresser and in the closet.

There's nothing that looks like it belongs to my parents, who could have checked in under any name and surely wouldn't put up pictures of themselves to decorate their hotel room.

I see a wallet on the nightstand and reach for it until I sense I'm being watched and shift quickly to straighten out the phone and notepad. But when I glance back at my coworker, sweat forming on her brow and cheeks reddened from exertion, I still get a dirty look.

"We're not supposed to touch guests' belongings," she says, a warning.

"I was straightening up," I say, which does nothing to alter her severe expression.

Dad wouldn't have a cheap brown-leather wallet like that anyway, and I start a mental list of rooms and check this one off.

Back in the hall, I chafe at both the risk of being watched and at the futility of aimlessly popping into rooms and hoping to find the one I'm looking for by chance.

On top of that, lying about the wallet brings what Wesley said back to mind. I keep saying I want to be honest but keep lying anyway. The desire to be different from him and prove him wrong burns deep.

I know I can change. I might change. One day, things will be easier, allowing me to change.

Am I lying to myself again? I refuse to believe so, but this habit is hard to break.

Having dumped the toilet paper between a few carts, I lurk the ground-floor hallways for help while this mental battle rages in my head. I feel like one more lie will kill me, but what would happen if telling the truth costs me and my sister everything?

Still carefully avoiding Sadie and the front desk but snooping around the internal staff areas, I stumble upon a small IT room, door open with a guy in his early thirties before a pair of computer monitors, some security feeds running through some nearby screens.

It's not until he swivels his chair to me and waves that I realize I've been gawking blankly at him amidst my mental contortions. If he's got access to the computer system, he must be able to tell me which guests belong to which rooms.

"Can I help you?" he asks, scratching his unshaven cheek.

"Yes!" I say, brightening up and stepping forward into the room as I realize I've told the truth, at least for one word. "I'm sorry to bother you, but I'm trying to figure out which room a particular pair of guests are in."

So far, so good, I think, practically holding my breath. If I can get through this one conversation without lying, maybe things can work out the way they should while proving I can change after all.

"What do you need that for?" he asks, eyeing my cleaning staff uniform.

It would be so easy to make up a story about them needing help with something or losing something, but this pressure in my head builds when I have difficulty articulating it. There's no way I can tell him that I want to go in and look through their bags.

"Are you OK?" he asks, squinting at me.

Oh no, I've taken too long.

"Yes, I am," I say, close enough to the truth to pass. "Sorry about that. I need to get in and check a room for these guests, but I don't know which one it is."

Smiling, I try to think if I didn't really answer his question and simply repeated myself from before. His slow nodding conveys his skepticism, and he leans back in his chair, showing me a beer gut hidden under a green t-shirt.

"The front desk can help you with that," he says, starting to turn away, and I panic.

"Wait, can you please? I'm new, and things didn't get off on the right foot with Sadie. I don't think she would like it if she saw me doing anything other than scrubbing a toilet."

To my surprise, the guy starts chuckling. "She's a real ball-buster, isn't she? Kind of acts like she owns the place."

"Yeah," I say, cautiously optimistic as he looks me over again. I'm not sure what he's looking for, but I hope I don't have to give him any truths he may not like.

"Alright, what are their names?"

I'm so excited that I immediately blurt out the answer. "I don't know...what names they're checked in under."

Phew, that was close.

The IT guy's expression sours, and he takes his fingers off the keyboard.

"You've got to give me something."

"I'm sorry," I say, apologizing for the third time. I try to think fast. "They checked in last Wednesday. One of the more expensive rooms on the top two floors. Man and a woman in their fifties."

His cringe continues, and I can see when his mouth cracks

open that he's about to tell me that's not enough. Worrying that I'm blowing it, I try to come up with more.

"Umm, they like to go for walks on the beach. The lady has hair that sweeps out around her shoulders. The man is relatively tall with a good tan and these colorful Hawaiian shirts. Maybe you've seen them on the security cameras? No. They flew in from Dallas."

Suddenly his eyebrows rise, putting an end to my rambling.

"When flights and hotel are booked at the same time, sometimes we do get that information for shuttle pickup purposes. Let me check," he says, beginning to type.

Out of the corner of my eye, I catch some movement that turns out to be Sadie stepping into the hallway. Quickly, I scoot inside and shut the door behind me. With the room so small, I end up right next to the IT guy's chair. This room has a lot of wires but not enough ventilation.

I turn my attention to the monitor, green letters on a black background, none of the nice interface of a website. It's impossible for me to make heads or tails of it.

"Anything?" I ask.

"I think I've got it," he says, and even hearing that makes my fingertips tingle. "A couple from Dallas, booked for a week in room 407."

I nearly gasp but instead ask, "And what are their names, so I know in case I run into them again?"

He nods, catching some of my infectious enthusiasm. "Vin and Elena Travikek."

"Brilliant," I say, bending over a little and throwing an arm over his shoulders. I'll probably need to wash it but am so happy that I don't care. And I made it through the entire conversation without a single lie. The world didn't end!

Twisting around to open the door, I stagger out when he calls to me from within his IT cave.

"Hey, I'm Paul Kimby. I didn't catch your name."

For the first time in a long time, I don't have to think to answer, and it feels like such a weight has been lifted off my shoulders.

"I'm Emily Marks."

19

S till celebrating my accomplishment of making it through one conversation without lying, I take the seashell-trimmed staircase to the fourth floor and breeze through the hallway, gazing ravenously at room 407 as I pass.

Another one of the cleaning ladies is a couple of doors down, and I startle her when I knock on the door.

"No need to be jumpy. It's only me. Here, I'll handle these rooms. Why don't you take a break?"

The lady wears a tan and gold uniform like mine, but her hair has some gray streaks sneaking in, and a couple of decades of this work are weighing down her eyebrows and cheeks. She looks at me like no one has ever suggested she take a break in her life.

There's no argument, which makes me happy until I realize that I need to finish cleaning this room and the next one before I can get to my parents' room and the treasure trove of incriminating evidence it's sure to contain.

But sometimes enjoying the anticipation of something is the best part, and with my goal so close at hand, I savor the accomplishment.

I spend a lot of time dreaming of what I might find there. Even something as simple as a photo ID of my parents masquerading as Vin and Elena Travikek would show a pattern of fraudulent behavior that should give my sister a reason to appeal her sentence. All I need to do is reveal that they're behind the Bedrock Ponzi scheme, and no one will be surprised that they got their start ripping off nursing home residents.

The room I'm in isn't particularly boring either, even if my mind is elsewhere. Condom wrappers in the trash, a collection of weird Troll dolls on the nightstand, waxing supplies in the bathroom, and an assortment of scuba equipment around the room point to some people living their best lives.

Hoping these oddities are only the appetizer, I rush through the room-cleaning routine I'm only vaguely familiar with. I change the sheets and towels, take out the trash, wipe down the surfaces, refill the toilet paper and bath supplies, and move on to the next room as quickly as I can.

It's a relief when I find that the next room over is mostly clean, almost like there's nobody in it, only a small personal bag and some bottles of nail polish by the sink. Definitely no hairless scuba sex going on here. Without any towels on the floor and the bed looking practically made already, I can't resist cutting some corners so I can get to the next room.

Pushing my cleaning cart in front of room 407 with a big smile on my face, I anxiously swipe my employee access card and listen to the click of the lock. The door swings open, revealing their luxurious room with the light coming in through the balcony doors on the other side.

I don't remember my parents' bedroom being very clean when I was growing up, and the state of this room strikes me as being a match—articles of clothing on the floor, wrappers and empty food containers around, bed practically torn apart.

Immediately, I spot three large, heavy-looking suitcases lined up by the wall near the closet and bathroom.

These aren't mere travelers; these are people on the run.

My smile widens, and I traipse into the room like it's all mine for the taking. The nightstand has some loose change on it, some receipts, and the usual Ritz guest materials. At first glance, I can't see anything specific that really screams it's my parents' room, but there's something about the smell that tells me it's theirs.

It's like the smell of a hair dryer left on way too long blowing on potpourri made of orange peels and fried chicken.

Now that this unpaid job has served its purpose, I banish any thought of cleaning in here. An unmade-up room will be the least of my parents' problems when I'm through with them.

Instead, I go ahead and close the door to give myself a little more privacy as I search for something that will help us. Perhaps I'll find some kind of bank statement pointing to where all their money is, making our fake bank irrelevant. I can't see Mom carrying that around with her while she's gallivanting around the seashore.

It's hard to know where to start, and in this fancy suite there are a lot of places to look—a full kitchen, a balcony looking out over the ocean, an alcove with a desk. This resort room is even larger than Miles's apartment.

After checking the receipts left out on the nightstand and seeing they're for simple toiletries from a drugstore, I let that guide me into the bathroom to quickly check that off my list. I can't imagine much documentation would be in here, but as I scan the room I spot something by the sink I get stuck on.

It's a porcelain duck that I recognize from our apartment in Dallas when I was growing up. Almost enough to make me rub my eyes and ask if it's really here, I marvel at something I remember fondly and haven't seen in probably eight years.

Oh, it was missing the last time I left our place, once I found out my parents had already left and weren't coming back. I'd thought the cute duck had been broken or thrown out, but apparently they took it with them. Taking the small figure in my hand, I feel a strange connection to a time in my life I'd never thought I'd want to remember.

Why do my parents still have this?

I can't dwell on it too long though and need to get down to business.

Next, I check dresser drawers and other cabinets, on the hunt for papers or tablets, notepads or brochures, anything that could point to what my parents have going on. A phone would be the jackpot, but there's nothing left out or hidden away anywhere.

I spot Mom's purse tucked close to the side of the bed, one that really does need to have the sheets cleaned for reasons I don't want to think about.

Brushing aside the usual junk, I find some cash and other stuff, but there's no ID or credit cards that would suggest how they're paying for things or where they're keeping their stolen money. Disappointed, I drop the bag on the floor and move on.

I'm starting to get anxious and know I can't avoid the luggage any longer.

Hustling over and pulling one down so that it's flat on the floor, I yank the zipper and rip the thing open, hungry to find something from Bedrock that they had to have taken with them.

Instead, what I find is a bag full of Dad's clothes, bottles of cologne, some liquor picked up at the airport duty-free shop, a few pairs of dress shoes, and his shaving items. The luggage doesn't even have an identifying tag on it, and I'm about to give up and move on when I glimpse something dull red at the bottom of the bag.

Nudging away some dress shirts, I get a better look at an old baseball hat I used to wear when I was younger. I'd played t-ball one year as a kid, and everyone had these hats with a ball and bat depicted on the front.

Gasping, I pull the hat out, in disbelief that I'm seeing this again. I'd been so excited about playing, and I'm able to focus on that now instead of all the bitter comments about having a girl on the team that caused me to quit and never play again.

Why would my dad still have this after all this time? I conclude it must have been thrown in by accident with some other stuff.

As much fun as I'm having finding things that remind me of my early years, I need something about Melanie, Bedrock, the stolen money, or the order to have me killed. And they're not in with my dad's stuff.

The next piece of luggage, a light-purple one, weighs twice as much as the first and contains all of Mom's things. The heft of it makes me think something good must be in here, but ripping it open reveals some kettlebells and other workout equipment and then a lot of clothes.

I get squeamish going through her clothes, especially when I realize how much of it is lingerie. And considering these garments don't have a lot of fabric to them, even the single eye-scalding glance I take suggests that there are probably fifty sets. Then there are curling irons, massage tools, and a lot of personal care items I couldn't care less about.

I glance back at the t-ball cap and am not surprise there's nothing similar in Mom's luggage, even if accidental. After what she said in her office and the heartless things she said to me growing up, I couldn't believe for a minute that she'd have a keepsake of my childhood around.

That leaves only one large suitcase, not particularly heavy but not empty either, and I'm salivating thinking that this is the business bag where they keep all of the paperwork for their heist and getaway.

But when I open it up, I'm speechless.

It's nearly full, but none of it is about their fraudulent business, brazen scam, or new identities.

No, this entire bag is full of things that are mine and Melanie's.

Toys, dolls, games, school papers, drawings, hair ribbons, cute girls' clothes, and more. Everything that as a kid I'd thought had seemingly disappeared or been thrown out as our apartment got more cramped and new stuff got brought in.

I'm so excited that I nearly dive into the bag, flipping through magazines, even finding a couple of little notes I'd written to Melanie when I was in fifth grade. Some of the glitter from an art project has rubbed off onto the suitcase's interior surface. I have found treasure in here, and I want to keep it all and pretend like I had the good childhood all of this stuff suggests.

"Oh my goodness!" I say out loud, despite no one else being here, when I unearth a Halloween costume from one year when I was Dorothy from *The Wizard of Oz*. It's filthy and ragged, but I squeeze it against my chest and laugh.

Unable to stop myself, I dig into one of the side pockets and find an old disposable camera. In addition to that, there are a handful of pictures in a pouch, and one of them is the exact same picture I've been carrying around of the four of us sitting together on the couch, Melanie waving the TV remote like a magic wand.

Discovering that hits too deep, and the fun I've been having gives way to choking up and tearful eyes.

Why is this the stuff my parents brought with them on their run from the law? I can't believe they even still have this.

What is it doing here? And if they cared enough to keep all

of this, why didn't they care enough to pay attention to me and Melanie and take good care of us when we were younger? Why run out on me and get my little sister thrown in jail for a crime they committed?

My hands lower to my thighs, unable to pick up another nostalgic item. There's a mirror set into the wall nearby, and I see my colored dark-brown hair. What's real: the childhood I want to imagine from these belongings, or the person I am now, doing so much to run from who I am?

Kind of seems like neither.

Much of my hungry zeal diminished, I find it much harder to continue my search, but there are so many more places to look, and I can't give up. My parents must be looking back at our years together with the same rose-colored glasses I am, imagining they were good parents who did the right thing, even though all evidence points to the contrary.

Inside a closet in the room, there is a safe, which very well may be the spot they're hiding everything that would be incriminating. Sighing, I wonder if I've wasted my time all along and this plan to quickly get a job here was futile to begin with.

None of the papers I found have a combination written down on them either. I start to wonder if as an employee I could get access to this somehow. Maybe that IT guy, Paul, could get it for me if I came up with a good reason for it. Now that would be a conversation in which lying would be unavoidable.

While I'm pondering what to do next and hoping this hasn't been a worthless endeavor, I hear voices in the hall. I dismiss them and keep looking until the voices hover around outside the door.

Jerking my head, I huff as I wonder if Sadie or another hotel-cleaning staff member has figured out I've been spending too much time here. Couldn't they leave me alone for ten more minutes?

Hastily, I lurch over to the bed and yank off one of the sheets, as if I'm about to make the bed, when I hear the keycard swipe and the lock click.

The door swings open, and of course I'm staring right at the doorway with the sheet in my hand, bent over like I'm hard at work.

It's not the cleaning-staff ladies. And it's not Sadie.

In walks Mom with Dad right behind her. The playful smile drops from her face as she recognizes me immediately. My dark hair does nothing to fool her when the face and body she saw only days ago are right in front of her.

All I can do is gape, speechless, as I think about the way she pointed her gun at me when she tried to blow me away.

Her eyebrows lower as her surprise gives way to outrage.

"Emily!"

20

S tricken by the sight of my parents, I panic and do the first thing that comes to mind. I try to run.

But with the two of them blocking the only doorway out of here, the best I can do is stagger back away from the bed in the direction of the balcony doors, the sun streaming in and wispy clouds in the sky beyond.

Since this is the fourth floor, a jump is out of the question, and so is scaling the building to try to get to another room. Cursing myself, I think that if I'd known my parents would be coming in, I would've hidden in the closet or bathroom and then tried to rush out with my face covered while their backs were turned.

Instead, Mom and Dad are focused right on me, inching closer with serious looks on their faces. Dad's tan has deepened significantly in the few days he's been here. Mom looks much different out of her business suit, especially up close.

Her eyes are fixed on me, unflinching but restrained, like I'm a bird she doesn't want to scare away before she can catch it.

She's still a tiny bit larger than me, though perhaps it's her hair making her seem that way. Regardless, she's slightly over twice my age and has already shown she has no qualms about doing whatever it takes to get what she wants, even if it means trying to kill me twice.

"Stay right there," she commands, her white skirt swaying as she creeps closer.

Her hands are empty, but it's her fixated eyes that appear the most dangerous. I've seen how quickly they can convey her rage and disappointment.

With them coming at me and leaving the doorway less guarded, I consider making a break for it and doing an end-run around them, hopping on the bed, and high-tailing it out of the room.

Now's my chance, but instead involuntarily I try to quickly steal another glance at the suitcase full of my things, inconveniently regretting that I can't take any of them with me. There's no way I'll ever be able to come back for that t-ball hat or the notes I sent my sister.

Mom takes advantage of my foolishly distracted state and lunges at me, hands with nails painted pink outstretched to tackle me. Gritting my teeth, I raise my forearms at the last second, wondering if Mom would really try to strangle me to death.

It's not her style. Anything more than pulling a trigger is too much work for her.

We collide, and I struggle to hold her off until I feel her arms wrap around me.

Wait a second, she's trying to hug me.

Abandoning my resistance, I stand there with my arms at my sides as my mother holds me close and even tilts her head to rest it on my shoulder, her dirty-blond hair brushing my cheek.

"Mom?" I ask, not sure what she's doing.

This is the woman who said I was her biggest mistake and that I ruin everything. The one who sent a girl to kill me and then pointed a pistol at me. Years of borderline neglect and emotional abuse in my early teen years, not to mention telling me my sister, Melanie, was dead when she'd merely been foisted off on a relative.

And now she's hugging me like she has any right to after what she's put me through.

I should push her away so hard that she falls over. My moment of vengeance could be right now.

But all I can do is stand there and accept the hug and the warmth, even if she doesn't deserve the chance to give either to me.

When she pulls away, she has both a bright smile and tears in her eyes, the kind of look a mother might reserve for a child's graduation or wedding day. It takes her a second to get her emotions under control while my dad's expression changes to a similar one of respect and satisfaction.

I don't understand. I've broken into their room and should be caught red-handed. They should be ripping me to shreds, knowing they're at risk of me exposing their scheme.

"I knew you'd make it," Mom says, struggling to keep her composure.

Instead, it's like they're happy to see me. Huh?

"What are you talking about?" I ask, bewildered, and Dad comes up beside Mom and wraps an arm around her shoulders, squeezing her close.

"I never had a doubt," he adds while looking at me with a satisfied half smile.

It's the kind of look a proud parent gives their kid, something I've never seen once from either of them.

I shake my head, wondering what's going on. My feeling is that this has to be some kind of trap. I should be running and thinking of my safety, but instead I'm letting my guard down and trying to figure out why they're behaving so strangely.

Mom releases a stilted sigh and wipes a tear from her cheek before reaching out to hold my shoulder. I stare at her hand on me and then follow the length of her arm.

The sensation comes to continue our argument in the office, demand they give back the money and get my sister out of jail, but the novelty of this parental affection wipes all of it from my mind.

"It wasn't difficult to find you," I say, unsure if I'm bragging or trying to rub it in.

Mom chuckles lightly. "I can't tell you how long I've waited for this moment. You made it," she says breathily.

"She's our girl. Of course she did," Dad adds, a twinkle in his dark-brown eyes, like he might tear up too.

I get the sense that I'm in the dark again and work up some indignation, crossing my arms and glaring at them.

"Would either of you like to tell me what you mean?"

They glance at each other and can't resist following up with a peck on the lips and putting their cheeks together as they gaze at me, not at all put off by my skepticism.

Mom covers her face in her hands, hunching over slightly. She appears to be gathering the courage for something.

"Oh, Emily, I know this has been a nightmare, but it's over now. All you had to do was prove yourself, and you came through with flying colors."

I squint at her, hearing everything she said yet still having trouble making sense of it.

Dad smirks and then bumps his hip against Mom's to get her attention.

"You're not explaining this clearly."

Mom shakes her head. "Does it really require an explanation?"

"Actually, yes!" I say impatiently, waving my arms. That

draws a slightly irritated look from Mom, more akin to what I'm used to.

She takes a deep breath and relaxes, again looking like a charming and gentle older lady who's inhabiting my mother's aging but svelte body.

"Look at what you've done. You've found your way back to us after overcoming adversity, surviving against the odds, and scraping by with nothing but your ingenuity. I'm so proud of you rising to the challenge!"

I release a long exhale. Every impulse in my body is telling me this is some kind of trap, that they're tricking me for something. This has to be an act.

"So what?"

Mom swallows and nods, tilting her head away to stare off into space for a moment.

"I know it's hard for you to understand, but I did all of this for you. It wasn't easy being detached and distant, but it was for your own good. The last thing we ever wanted was for you to be weak and needy, an incapable, floundering mess like so many other kids these days. Look at how independent and strong you are. It makes all of the sacrifices worth it."

A sharp laugh escapes my lips. I don't know what kind of crazy story she's been telling herself, but it is pure fantasy.

"Are you kidding me? Are you trying to say that you two ignored me growing up and then left me before I'd even graduated from high school so that you could toughen me up?"

Even though I've stopped talking, my mouth is still open in pure disbelief.

Dad sets his jaw, his begrudging smile still there.

"One day you'll understand. It's hard for you to see it now, because this is naturally who you are, but you needed to be set on this path," he says.

"And now we can keep going on it together," Mom picks up

instantly. "It'll take time for the grievances you have against us to fade, but you're still in your early twenties. We have the rest of your life to be supportive parents and a model family, together."

What? Mom and Dad really need to stop trying to influence my life with these elaborate, yearslong schemes!

My head is spinning.

21

Mom nods, like I'm supposed to simply accept that we're a happy family now and forget about everything I lived through, but I feel like I'm on the verge of a nervous breakdown. *No, just no.* They were neglectful, emotionally abusive parents.

I'll never forget the time Mom told me about the only thing I was good for and that I should head out on the street. I was sixteen years old when she said that.

And that's far from the only thing that flies in the face of whatever tough lesson they imagine they were teaching me.

"Mom, it wasn't even one week ago when you pulled a gun out of your purse, pointed it at me, and pulled the trigger."

She cocks her hip and gives me a condescending look, her wingtips bouncing.

"Do you really think I would miss from the other side of the room, unless it was intentional? Come on."

Gasping, I go to the next example that comes to mind.

"You sent Alice Patterson to kill me. You hired and paid for someone to murder me!" I shout. If the meaning of what I'm saying doesn't get through to them, the volume should.

But neither Mom nor Dad are the least bit perturbed.

"Emily, please, if I really wanted you dead, would I send a stuck-up girl from the human resources department to do it?"

Dad chuckles, scratching his midsection. "If you couldn't beat her, maybe you would've deserved it."

I shake my head hard. "She died because of what you did!"

I'm so caught up in my own disoriented head that I don't notice my mom move until she's set her hand on my shoulder, forcing eye contact with me.

"Don't feel bad about it. She was chosen for a reason, one you already know. She actually had a handful of people who were her literal slaves, but they're free now. No one will miss her, and no one cares that she's gone."

I try not to think about the call from the McCurtain County Sheriff's Office demanding that I talk to them. They know I'm involved, and the guilt eats away at me.

I thought my parents were evil. They may still be, but they're definitely also crazy.

"OK, forget Alice—"

"See, that proves our point. Not even you care about her," Dad interrupts.

I flinch. "I do care about her," I insist, too emotional to try to sort out if that's a lie or not. "But what about Melanie? She's in jail because of something you did. Her entire twenties are going to be spent in a women's prison. We were never able to be there for each other in our teens, having the kind of girls' time we deserved."

Mom at least has the decency to sigh, but then it comes with a shrug.

"We don't play favorites between our children. Melanie is getting the same lessons you did, and soon enough we'll all be together."

I scoff, feeling like I need to sit down. The insanity and the gall and the disbelief are too much to take.

"Are you saying you made me spend five years alone on the streets of Dallas and put Melanie in prison for the last five years so that we would grow up to be independent, strong women?"

"Yes!" both Markses shout in unison, beaming as if I finally got it.

And now I do need to sit down. Luckily there's a bed right nearby I can spill against. Elbows on my knees, I rub my face and glare at them.

"Do you honestly expect me to believe any of that?" I shout, although I'm not nearly as harsh as I could be.

It isn't lost on me that I'm still basically trapped in their room and at their mercy. If this is a trick, and Mom's planning to pull a gun on me again anyway, or if she wants me to go along with this, throwing too much cold water on it could make them angry and me dead.

We still need to get all of the stolen money out of them, and that'll never happen if they figure out I'm not merely here to find them, that in fact I was with the pair outside on the deck when my name slipped out.

Mom has her hands clasped in front of her, bright fingernails flashing in the sunlight coming in through the balcony doors.

"I know it'll take time to regain your trust and make you understand. You have bad memories from hard days when we weren't there for you. But you're exactly where you're supposed to be, and we'll all be able to grow together and be a perfect family now."

Now that she's mentioned being together a second time, it teases out something that irks me. It doesn't make sense for an entirely new reason.

"But how could that even be possible when Melanie is still in prison?" I say.

Dad tips over and spills onto the bed next to me, like we're a normal family that is comfortable around each other. Arm propping up his head while on his side, he looks at me with a debonair smile.

"We break her out. All it takes is paying off a few of the right people, and she can walk right out. It'll take a lot of money, but we have even more."

I shake my head, not able to fathom if that's a real possibility or not. No, the only way she gets out is if my parents go in or otherwise are proven responsible.

But that's only the beginning of the absurdity of what kind of family life my parents are imagining we're now on the brink of.

"And then be together where? You two are on the run, and Melanie would've broken out of prison and can't be out in open society. I'm basically in hiding too. What are you saying we're supposed to do?"

Mom raises her arms and smirks, like it's obvious.

"Other than the States, we can go wherever we want and do whatever we want. There's a big world out there. No reason to get hung up on one country. We have enough money to stay in resorts like this our entire lives if that's what we want," she says.

I nod despite seeing the obvious gaps in their perverse logic.

"Right, you created your company and robbed millions of people so that we'd have plenty of money to survive after Melanie and I endured our hardships and became empowered adults. Do I have that right?"

My parents share another look before breaking out into laughter. Mom spills into bed beside Dad and rolls to him. Dad instinctively wraps his arm around her and pulls her close. They kiss, and I remember these sheets haven't been changed.

I stand up and take a few steps away, wondering if I should bolt for the door. But I kind of want to see what else they've dreamed up in their heads.

"No, getting the money was for us. That's our lives' work.

Setting you two straight has been more like a side project," she says, eyes widening when she sees I start to take offense. "But that's all parenting is anyway, another aspect of our lives. Doesn't hurt for one part to help out the other part now that our family is getting back together again."

Unless you've been robbed of your life savings, I think.

I cross my arms, not sure what to make of this but knowing I'll never be able to sort it all out in the spur of the moment. At least I have the sense they're not going to strangle me or throw me off the balcony...for now.

Straining, I struggle to figure out if they are for real or if what they're talking about would even be possible. There's some discomfort in the pit of my stomach that I'm afraid to touch.

"We would always be on the run from people looking for us. It would never be safe to use our names," I say.

Mom's placid smile is probably meant to be comforting but instead exacerbates my dismay.

"I've always said you can be anything you want. That includes having any name you want. Make up the person you've always dreamed of being, be that, and love every minute of it," she says, sitting up alongside Dad, who still has his arm around her. She sets her hand on his knee.

But what if all I want is to be Emily Marks without having to lie or be ashamed of it?

Shutting my eyes, I shake my head. This is another trick, a con job they came up with as soon as they saw me. No, they're finally telling the truth, and this is my ticket to the happy family I've always wanted.

I can't decide what's real, and I open my mouth, unsure what will come out of it.

"I...have to think about this," I mutter, my head feeling like it's going to split in two.

After noticing Mom nod calmly, the opposite of when she'd

yell and scream when I wouldn't do whatever she wanted, I glance at the suitcase full of my childhood things.

Dad gets up and guides me to the door. It opens, and the cleaning cart is still there, not that I'll ever touch it again.

Before I can leave, he tugs on my cleaning uniform sleeve, drawing me back.

"We know you'll need time to realize we're serious," he says, and the loving warmth drains from his face, revealing a momentary icy glare. "But don't even think about turning us in."

22

I stagger down the stairs, grab my things from the employee area, and head toward the main entrance, passing Sadie and the reception desk on the way out.

"And where do you think you're going?" she howls, wheeling around the desk to chase after me and already getting red in the face, but my mind is using so much processing power trying to figure out what my parents are up to. I can hardly even perceive that she's around me.

"I'm done," I mumble, dropping the cleaning uniform right there on the floor and turning away.

She continues to screech like a banshee, but none of it makes it into my head as I clear the doors and head out to the street.

My walk back to our Airbnb proceeds like a zombie's aimless march, my brain and my feet completely disconnected. Do my parents really think I could forgive them for what they've done? I loathed being Alice for just one day, so could I bear being someone else for the rest of my life? Would I do it if it meant getting my sister back?

Worst of all is the uncomfortable sensation I get when I

consider their main point. Did I somehow benefit personally from being dirt poor and desperate from when I was seventeen years old?

I'm reminded of Miles saying that they shouldn't underestimate how strong I am. Did they actually somehow do something to engineer how I am?

And then there's Dad's cold threat about if I did something to act against them.

I can't even begin to scratch the surface of everything by the time I reach our place, which now has the sign above the front for Greater Cayman Bank.

Miles has been busy, and I can't forget that even entertaining the idea of having my family back together would mean crushing Miles's hopes of helping my parents' victims.

Stepping inside the cool, air-conditioned space, I see how some well-placed items have made this commercial-space-turned-residential unit into the kind of low-key office one might expect to be running on a tropical island.

A few flyers, another sign, Miles's laptop arranged on the top of the counter. Since I have no idea what a Cayman Islands' bank looks like, I have to imagine this could easily pass as one.

It's not until I round the counter, reach the stairs near the back, and hobble up them that I find Miles, who is fixing himself a sandwich in the kitchenette. Wherever Taylor and Wesley are, together or apart, it's not here.

I nearly gasp at Miles, like I didn't expect him to be here in the place where we're staying, and he gives me a strange look like he can immediately tell that I'm out of sorts. A part of me wants to curl up in his arms and forget the world, but I'm used to toughing it out and dealing with things on my own.

He puts the finishing touches on the sandwich, some mustard on the top slice, and puts it together before pushing the plate to me. I nearly collapse and could kiss him for that.

It's as close as I'll get to being able to curl up into a ball right now.

The sandwich is mediocre, but I'll keep that opinion to myself and try to savor the sweetness of him giving it to me. The moment reminds me of when we were in his apartment.

"How did it go?" he asks gently, leaning across the table near the kitchen. Despite his natural tan, he looks a little red, either from the sun or the effort, probably having been as busy as me.

"Good," I say simply, and he stares at me like that didn't count as an answer. "OK, things started off fine when Wesley and Taylor followed my parents out onto the deck and had their easily overheard conversation about our bank, but then the two of them got into a fight, basically breaking up right in front of Mom and Dad. So I don't know if they'll want to take their financial advice after that."

Setting his butter knife down, Miles takes a seat and rubs his forehead. When he gives me a listless look, I can tell he really wants to say "I told you so" about Wesley and Taylor but is holding himself back.

Maybe they did ruin everything and should have been left behind. At least Mom and Dad didn't seem to know I was with them.

Miles purses his lips, like he's trying to swallow a bitter pill.

"It was a good idea anyway," he says at last, being much kinder about my plan than I deserve. "We might have no choice other than to go ahead and call the authorities and hope for the best."

I nod despite feeling some surprising reluctance. A few hours ago, I would've been completely fine with that, but now after what happened, I'm not so sure.

"That's not all though. Later, when I was cleaning, I was able to get into their room and look around."

He perks up, coming back to life quickly.

"And?" he says, eager. "Did you find out what their plans are?"

I glance away, not ready to share what they said about wanting me back in their lives. Miles would say it was a cheap ploy, making me feel foolish for getting hung up on it for a single second.

"They didn't have anything around suggesting what they were up to," I say, ostensibly true, "though perhaps there's something in a safe. I did get their current fake names though."

"That's something. Do you want to call the police, or should I?"

My eyes widen, and I feel put on the spot. Is simply turning them in going to give us the best chance of recovering the money and helping Melanie? Before, Miles didn't think the money might ever surface this way, but perhaps he thinks it's a lost cause.

He watches me, waiting and expecting an answer.

Too bad I don't have one for him.

Before I can come up with what to say, we hear the front door downstairs open and close quickly, the sounds of footsteps following.

With a sheepish grin, I get up from the table, though I'm barely able to turn around before we see Taylor march up the stairs. Miles immediately furrows his brows, but I put my hand on his arm to hold him back.

It's unlikely he'd snap at her, but he doesn't know the whole story or who's really at fault. She gives us a cursory glance, enough for me to see she's still hurt. Did I look like that after breaking up with Wesley? I try not to think about it.

"Hey, do you want something to eat? We're having sandwiches," I say, and she reflexively shakes her head.

"I think I'm going to find a beach to hang out on," she says.

"That's a good idea," I say.

Taylor glances back at the bedroom she'd been sharing with Wesley and starts toward it only to stop at the doorway.

"He's gone, and I don't think he's coming back. It looks like he's taken his stuff, most of it at least."

Miles and I exchange a glance. Wesley gone, just like that? I should feel relieved and at most not care, but tell that to the sinking feeling in my gut.

"He'll be able to take care of himself," I say, and Taylor turns back to us, leaning against the doorframe.

"You probably think I'm stupid for being into him," she says, sighing.

"No, having him vanish isn't how I wanted this to end. I feel like I've failed because somehow through all of this I wasn't able to help him break his habit," I say.

Taylor gives me a wry smile.

"A habit? Is that what we're calling it now?"

Miles smirks, and I suppose I deserve being called out on it. I can't believe I'm still giving Wesley the benefit of the doubt.

"The way all three of us have been living can seem like it's set in stone, but I'm learning that it's a choice we've been automatically making. We feel desperate, and we use that to justify doing whatever we want to other people," I say.

It startles me when I notice Miles listening intently. I don't think I was saying anything special.

Taylor shrugs.

"Bedrock was my lifeline to actually getting beyond the scams and even OnlyFans, but it's gone now, and so is Wesley. Now I have nothing."

That hits me hard, and I shake my head emphatically.

"That's not true. You have a lot going for you, and we're all going to get through this and figure something out."

Thankfully, some light flickers in Taylor's eyes as she snaps out of her funk.

"You're right. I do have a killer bathing suit I've been waiting to try. Maybe I'll enjoy being in it for myself and not even take pictures," she says, looking excited as she turns into her room.

I laugh and am a little jealous that she's able to show off at the beach now that her part is done.

"Try not to break too many hearts today!" I call as she closes the door to change.

That leaves me and Miles together again, and he crosses his arms in a thoughtful way, giving me a glimpse of some definition around his shoulders and collarbone. Bulging muscles are nice, but there's still plenty to appreciate about Miles's body, the way he carries himself, his dark-brown eyes.

"I wonder what I'll be doing next," he says airily.

I know he's talking about work, but I can't let this chance go to make my case again after last night's missed connection. I've definitely been too hands-off with him, as we focused on holding my parents accountable, and I wouldn't mind being more hands-on as soon as possible.

"I've got some ideas for things we could do," I say, my index finger grazing his wrist.

It's been a while since we kissed, and I couldn't be clearer about wanting more if I made a sign for it and hung it over the front door.

His thoughtful look continues, though it is directed at me now. A moment passes, and I realize I'm biting my tongue.

"Alright," he says plainly.

Let down by his lack of enthusiasm, I nod and try not to do anything to make this as awkward for him as it is for me. "Alright." Seriously? What about, "Oh really, like what?" Or better yet, "I've got some ideas of my own."

But he's distracted by this problem with my parents that I've forced on to him, and now I can see it's costing me Miles's attention and interest.

"OK," I say, hoping he'll be in a better place for us later.

When later will come is anybody's guess. Unless I'm ready to turn my parents in, trying to arrange another encounter with them seems hopeless.

I'd rather not think about suffering another apathetic rejection and finding myself in Taylor's shoes, not feeling like I have very much of anything going for me either.

Miles drifts away to his phone, and I think about spilling onto the couch or perhaps getting a postcard for Melanie... sending it once I have some good news for her.

Instead I hear Miles gasp, making me turn.

"What is it?" I ask.

His look of astonishment is so cute and warm that it could melt ice.

"The bank website got a hit, and there's a message. Your parents want to come, today!"

23

Despite screwing everything up, somehow Wesley and Taylor still came through. My parents got curious about our bank and want to talk about opening up an account. Leave it to Mom and Dad to tune out a messy breakup and seize an investment tip.

The look of wonder on Miles's face is mesmerizing, and I'm so excited that I'm shaking. My plan is working, at least this far.

"I have to get ready," Miles says, stepping in one direction and then doubling back the other way to go to his room.

I follow him anxiously, trying to imagine if this could actually get us back the money my parents stole from everyone. I barely have the mental capacity to try to weigh that against my father's threat.

I don't know how I could take my parents up on their offer and live a lie for the rest of my life. At the same time, I don't want them trying to kill me for real if they were merely doing it for sport before.

Even if Mom and Dad transfer all their ill-gotten gains into our bank account, they don't have to know they don't have control of it right away, right? That could give me time to figure out what to do.

Mostly, after getting us this far, I'm frantically trying to think of what I can do to make this succeed. It feels like everything is happening right now.

I follow Miles into his room, where he strips down to his boxers right in front of me and starts fishing for dressier clothes in his suitcase. I'm so frazzled that I'm barely able to relish what I'm looking longingly at.

"I know. While you're talking to them, I'll come in with a hat pretending to be another customer. Or I could be another employee and just talk on the phone in the background, making it seem like a real business. What about if I call you during your meeting, and you can put them on to talk to me. I know I can convince them to do it."

My chattering continues until Miles hops over with one leg in a pair of slacks. He looks me firmly in the eyes, and my shoulders slump. I know what he's going to say.

"You can't do any of that," he says, and I sigh. "They'll spot you."

I shake my head, my firmly ingrained sense of needing to do everything myself taking over again in this crucial moment. Did my parents program that into me too when they forced me to live on the street?

"But...but we have to make this work. This is the chance we've been waiting for. All that money could be lost if we don't convince them to hand it over."

Even though I'm in a tizzy and Miles looks nervous, he gives me a sympathetic look and sets his hand on my shoulder.

"It's got to be me," he says uneasily.

I'm nodding slowly, but my mind is going a mile a minute with all of the ways this could go wrong. It's doubtful Miles would accidentally bring me up in the conversation, like bone-head Wesley did, but he has his own issues as well.

It would be easier to push Miles out there and hope for the best, but I can see in his eyes that this is hard for him. I know he wants to get the stolen money back, but there are things he won't do.

"You're going to have to convince them it's a safe investment that will be good for them," I say solemnly.

He gives me a plaintive look. "I know," he says, agitated.

His eyebrows are furrowed, and he's having trouble buttoning his shirt. I step forward and start buttoning it for him, leaving his hands free to rub his head in dismay.

As I see him squirm, the thought hits me that this is too much for him. He helped other people who'd been overcharged, but he never had to participate in a ploy like this to get their money back.

He's in uncharted territory, and the thought strikes me to call it off. Maybe I should tell Miles to forget about it and keep living in his black-and-white world where he can always be the honest guy he is at heart.

On the other hand, if I can make it through one whole conversation without lying, I'm sure he can survive one too, even if it is with my manipulative parents.

"All you need to do is be friendly and professional, like you were going to be at Bedrock. If it gets tough, I want you to remember that my parents cost you your job too, even if you were quitting simultaneously. This is our one chance to get back the money they took before it vanishes within the global financial system."

He looks at me warily, and I can't tell if his resolve is strengthening or weakening. His eyes relax, viewing me in a way that seems exposed and vulnerable, like we're seeing each other for the first time.

"You would've made a good financial planner," he says, making me smirk.

I button one more button, there.

He looks at me like he's expecting to be thanked for the compliment, but I have a much better way to show my appreciation.

I lean in and press my lips against his. When I see his eyes pop open, I know that I caught him off guard. He's unsure at first but warms up to it, and I have to pull away before things get out of hand. I'll pass on my parents wandering up here looking for Miles and catching the two of us.

My close-lipped grin makes me embarrassed, and I'm playing with my fingers in front of me, though I can tell that even the kiss couldn't wipe Miles's nerves out completely.

"You'll do fine. You were begging to meet my parents, right?"

Eyebrows raised, he shakes his head.

"I don't think any guy has ever met a girl's parents like this," he mutters, releasing a pent-up sigh.

All I can do is put on a hopeful face as he turns to do his best with saving the world from my parents. He walks across the living room and turns down the stairs, giving me one apprehensive look before disappearing into Greater Cayman Bank's headquarters.

I take a seat at the top of the stairs where I can listen while keeping out of sight. At least this time I don't have to pretend to be cleaning anything.

Ten minutes later, I hear the door open and know it can only be my parents. Taylor has already left, and it sure isn't Wesley coming back.

"You are tucked away deep in here. I didn't think I could get lost on an island this small, but you nearly had us!" Dad chuckles.

"Getting here is half the challenge," Miles replies.

Dad's boisterous enthusiasm raises my optimism, but he's always been the charmer with an easygoing manner. He's never been the tough customer Miles would have to convince. I find myself holding my breath, knowing what's coming.

"Seems a little bare bones in here, wouldn't you say?" Diedre says. "I hope the quality of the decor doesn't reflect your service."

I shut my eyes even though I can't see them. It seems to take way too long for Miles to answer.

"You must be the couple looking at opening an account with us," Miles says smoothly. "Let me ask you this. What would you prefer a bank put its resources into, fancy furnishings or properly handling funds?"

"That's a good point," Dad says, and I exhale in relief.

I can only imagine that Miles's definition of properly handling funds involves returning them to the victims, but unless he's winking at them, my parents would never know that.

He's being honest and letting my parents make their own assumptions. Brilliant!

"OK then, so tell us about your operation," Mom demands. "How come I've never even heard of Greater Cayman Bank?"

A million things to say, all of them lies, spring to mind, but all I can do is cross my arms and hope that Miles comes up with something good.

"Sorry, how many Cayman Islands banks were you familiar with before coming here? We are relatively new but have a strong mission statement and a dedication to doing right by people. There are reasons people come here for their banking needs, often to avoid entanglements with the American financial system, and that's entirely your business. We don't ask, and you don't tell."

That puts a smile on my face. Miles is cleverer than I thought he was, saying things about the Cayman Islands that are true but have nothing to do with us or what we'd do with their money if we got our hands on it.

Some muttering between Mom and Dad follow that I can't entirely make out.

"So what are the advantages that account holders have?" Dad asks, more serious now and making my nerves reignite.

I know Miles isn't going to lie about giving them interest or making investments.

"We bring a lot of financial and investment know-how to the table, and I want you to know that if you do want to create an account and initiate a deposit with us, we'll immediately begin putting your funds to good use. The rewards are substantial. We know it took a lot for you to make your money, and you deserve to pay for it," he says.

My eyes widen, and I hear Miles cough.

"Did you mean, *get* paid for it?" Mom asks.

"My point is we're providing a service and benefits that no one else does, whether on the Cayman Islands or elsewhere. I can show you our marketing materials and brochures, if you'd like," he says quickly, some strain creeping into his voice that I hope only I can detect.

It feels like his slip has put us on thin ice.

"I don't need that," Mom says sternly, "but I do want to know our money will be safe with you, no matter what kind of investments or loans you make."

Some weak laughter from Miles follows, and I can tell the avenues are closing for making ostensibly helpful statements that are still true.

"You can rest easy knowing your money will be exactly where it's supposed to be," he says, sounding more confident.

"Will we have access to it anytime?"

As the questions get more pointed, I find myself cringing. Why can't they just say yes, hand over all their money, and leave without putting Miles through this? I can only imagine how he's dealing with this after all the discomfort he had simply with the idea of having this conversation with my parents.

"You will have access to the account for as long as it's active," Miles says hesitantly.

"But our money, how difficult is it if we need to make a withdrawal?"

"Most transfers take one to three business days."

"I think we've got it," Dad says, speaking up. "Forgive the twenty questions. We are talking about a substantial sum here."

"I'm not finished though," Mom says quickly, before I can start to feel like the worst is over. "One more question so we can be absolutely certain. Will we be putting our money in a secure, private account where we'll be guaranteed permanent access to it?"

Paling, my hands drop from my face to my lap. Leave it to my mom to ask such a specific question, leaving Miles no room for half-truths or peripheral information.

The impulse hits me to stand up and go down there, because I know the only answer Miles will possibly utter will be no. Then it'll all be over, my parents will walk out, and the stolen money will be gone.

Maybe this was a bad plan, one doomed to fail. Miles never should've been put in this role that he never could've pulled off. My parents didn't even ask any complicated financial questions. Taylor would've said yes without a second thought, lying through her teeth, no qualms about it.

A sinking feeling in my gut intensifies, and I think all hope is lost, but then Miles answers.

"Yes."

I'm shocked at hearing something I never thought I would. Miles lied.

24

As soon as I hear the door swing shut, I have to hold on to the railing to keep from bursting up. I only make it to the count of ten before I can't contain my excitement anymore and rush down the stairs, leaping the last few steps and swinging around toward the front of the building.

Miles, this amazing man I happened to meet when he replaced me at Bedrock, is standing there with a dumbstruck look on his lightly tanned face. I fling my arms wide and collapse against him, making him stagger back a step as he catches me.

Feeling his warmth against me is good, but what we accomplished is even better.

"Oh my goodness, Miles, you did it!" I say, giddy.

It's felt like there's been so much bad news and negativity that it's hard to believe something could actually go right. I laugh for no particular reason, light on my toes.

"Yeah, they went for it," he says, still managing to keep a mostly straight face, but I want him to let loose with me and feel the exhilaration of the moment.

Gazing at him in wonder that I hope will spark more

emotion from him, I ask, "How much did they transfer? I couldn't really hear."

He shakes his head and looks away, like he can't believe it himself.

"A lot," he mutters.

"How much?"

"An awful lot."

"Come on. Do I have to twist it out of you?" I say, taking his hand and tugging on it as if to twirl him around, but he doesn't budge.

"About seven hundred and fifty million dollars."

I look at him to see if he's really being serious. Those dark eyebrows and brown eyes, his hair still messy. Yes, very serious. In fact, way too serious when we should be delirious.

"Are you kidding me? Three-quarters of a billion dollars?" I gasp, staggering nearly to the point of losing my balance. "Can you imagine we have that much money, even for one single day before we immediately give it back?"

Despite the torrent coming out of my mouth, he's still stunned, and I think I understand why. It is a huge amount of money, more than anyone should ever have really, more than I could dream of, and the sum total of everything my parents have stolen from people all over the country.

"It's definitely something," he mumbles, and I see him grow increasingly sour.

It strikes me for the first time that he's not merely shocked or in awe of what he did. No, he's not happy about it, and no amount of me cajoling him, complimenting him, or showering him with affection is going to fix it.

"Think about all of the people you've helped. Everyone is going to get their money back, and only a matter of days after it went missing. This is a historic achievement, a personal legacy that many people fight their entire careers for only a fraction of. I thought you would be thrilled."

He looks at me blankly at first, emotionless, but then his eyes narrow slightly.

"It shouldn't have had to be this way," he says, subtly shifting onto his back foot.

I cross my arms. My euphoria wasn't contagious, but his discontent definitely is.

"I know this made you uncomfortable, but you said it yourself that this was the best way, and now we have the power to set this right. One little lie, one word, was good for seven hundred and fifty mil and millions of victims saved. Isn't that worth it?" I ask, my sky-high emotional state dropping like a stone.

"And now I'm in possession of stolen property," he says.

My mouth drops open, and I shake my head, never taking my eyes off him.

"But, Miles, we're going to give it right back. No one would ever fault you for this. You're not going to be arrested or in trouble. You're the hero here. And you've saved me too. This makes a world of difference to me," I say desperately, searching his face for any sign that I'm getting through to him.

But it's like he's wearing a mask, leaving me unable to see him, and he doesn't want to see me. Unmoved, he glances around the first floor of our fake bank and puckers his lips like he's sucking on a lemon.

"Do you know why honesty is so important to me? I've learned a lot about you, but I don't think you've learned much about me. Mostly because you've never asked."

That hits hard, and something inside me feels like it's breaking.

"Then please tell me!"

He releases an aggrieved sigh, as if he's feeling put upon for answering the question he essentially demanded I ask.

"When I was younger, thirteen or so, I was probably the most amoral person you've ever met. Even worse than Wesley. I'd lie about anything for no reason to anyone. I had no power, and bending the truth like that made me feel like I had control of something.

"There was one time when my parents got on my case that I was mountain biking through people's yards. One time I happened to fall on my way to school and had a cut on my arm. Somebody asked me about it, and I said my dad did it."

"Miles..."

He holds up his hand. "Not only were my parents investigated and tormented for months, my dad ended up losing his job as well. And do you know what they did? They never once asked me why I said that or even told me they were disappointed. No, they went on with me as if nothing had happened, trying to accept me and support me as best they could in ways that were perfectly reasonable.

"What they accepted was that I wasn't a trustworthy person, that I was someone who might hurt them badly. They didn't have to say they were disappointed, because I realized I was disappointed in myself and didn't want to be like that. I promised myself I'd be better and have been ever since, until today."

I want to reach out and hug him again but know it isn't the right time. My heart aches for him and what he experienced, but doesn't the good we're doing count for something?

"Miles, I'm so sorry that happened, but look at how much you've learned and grown since then. You made up for that lie times a billion with this one. And as truthful as you've been, we all tell half-truths and fudge the facts sometimes. It's human nature. Even the other things you said to my parents—"

"I lied more than once. You're right," he says sharply, pouring salt in my wound.

"No, that's not my point!"

Scowling, he steps away, and I inch forward, but he shifts and veers off when I want to be closer and make this better. Here we are in the most beautiful place having the ugliest moment. I'm sorry he didn't live up to his personal standard today, but I have to believe that one day he'll be OK with what he did.

"Let's talk about this more later when we're back in Dallas. Our flight is tomorrow morning. If my parents discover their money is all gone, they might be willing to figure something out that helps my sister," I say.

He shakes his head and casts a sidelong glance at me.

"I can't handle one more scheme or any kind of deal involving money that needs to go back at the first possible instant. This isn't what I want in my life," he says, and I know that the core of what he means is me.

I fight back tears.

"I told you when we first met..." I stop myself, trying to catch my breath. "Do you think I want this either? I know I'm a piece of work, but I've been killing myself to be better. I want to give up bad habits and live in a more honest way. We're so close. You inspire me to want to be a person with integrity, but I need a little more time."

Deep down, I knew this day would come and he'd get fed up with me.

"I can't wait that long," he says, and I don't know if he's talking about me or the flight or what, but regardless, he turns to leave.

Where he's going or what he'll do, I have no clue, but Miles simply shoulders open the door and steps out onto the small street in the heart of George Town, setting off with his hand in his pocket like he's any old tourist.

25

That leaves me alone at our Airbnb on a hot late afternoon, trying to think of how I can get myself in a suitable state to try to force my parents to admit guilt in Melanie's case over stolen money that neither of us have.

But the cold, dead feeling inside paralyzes me. I've prided myself on being so tough that I could make it through anything, but now I can barely move from this seat in the entryway, like I'm the next customer in line waiting for a representative from Greater Cayman Bank.

The door swings open, and I nearly snap my neck looking up in the hope that Miles has returned, but instead it's Taylor. She notices me slumped to the side and stops on a dime, lifting her large sunglasses.

There's some sand stuck to her thigh, and around her hairline and on her arms there's evidence that she got a lot of sun this afternoon.

"You look like a wreck," she says.

My only response is to sit up a little, and she comes over and flops onto the seat beside me. A silent moment drags as she looks around, no doubt noticing that I'm the only one here.

She finally circles around back to me and in a low voice says, "Did you catch some feelings?"

I nod reluctantly. That's one way to put it. Taylor sighs and leans back. If asked, I'd say I'd prefer to be alone, but I have to admit I'm comforted by her presence, even if she did try to kill me.

"Do you want to tell me what happened?"

I peer at her, feeling like I don't have another choice.

"After my parents left, Miles and I got into an argument in which he said some surprising things and then took off."

Taylor takes her glasses off and taps them on her chin, leaning forward and glancing back at me.

"Ahh, he told you that he's actually in love with me," she says.

I laugh despite myself. As painful as this is, it's hard to say if this is any worse than what Taylor went through with Wesley this morning. And somehow she's still standing.

Amazed at how a little laughter can resuscitate my mood, I give Taylor a careful look. Stringier and a bit shorter than me, she really isn't the thirsty floozy I first thought she was, even if there is a crazy streak somewhere in there.

"You know, you can be witty sometimes," I say.

She smiles wanly, relaxed.

"Thanks, but it's really only a good eye for irony."

Accepting her modest reply to my compliment, I lean forward to rub my legs and try to lean into packaging these feelings so I can wrap them up, set them aside, and figure out what to do next.

"He had to tell my parents a lie to get them to transfer their money to him, specifically that it would be guaranteed to be safe and accessible to them. I've been trying so hard to be more honest, but I'm starting to see that being rigidly truthful at all times is unrealistic and often unhelpful. Yes, it's good to be trustworthy within reason, but I think it's more being responsible that matters."

Taylor gives me a careful appraisal while my mind starts to drift to all of the irresponsible things I've done recently, some of which also include her. I purse my lips. I'm going to have to live with myself and keep striving to do better, without beating myself up if I slip.

"It sounds like there are some things he should learn from you," she says, and I crack a grin.

When I'd first met Miles, I had him eating out of the palm of my hand. Then when I needed him to help with my parents, the shoe shifted to the other foot. Now I feel like I can be myself again.

It's possible the only time I'll see Miles again is on the plane ride home. It would hurt, because there's still a lot to admire about him inside and out, but I'm going to keep going with my life, no matter who wants to be in it.

Right now, there's only one person in that category, the acquaintance turned frenemy turned enemy turned rival turned teammate next to me. I've always thought we had some similarities, and it's possible we may make it out of this actually being friends.

"Hey, the sun is setting. Why don't we head out and look for a bite to eat or something?" I propose.

She cocks an eyebrow and then hops out of her seat.

"I sure didn't come here to lock myself in our rental the whole time."

Grinning, I get to my feet too. We spend some time touching ourselves up in the bathroom and then set out into the dusky early evening, warm but cooler and definitely refreshing.

Even though my attire isn't anything to write home about, I feel clean and can hold my head up.

"Are we looking for trouble?" I ask Taylor, who's wearing a

short dress with spaghetti straps, as we cruise down the sidewalk.

It's hard to tell where to go since we're not that familiar with the island, but we see some other people out and about and naturally follow them toward the shore.

We end up at a beachside bar with glowing lights and lanterns overlooking the sand, surf, and sun dipping below the horizon in the distance. Much different from Three Tequila Floor or The Watering Hole, though this place doesn't have so much as a sign to display its name.

I'm here to have fun and forget about everything I've gone through for a while, which shouldn't be hard considering there are plenty of twenty-somethings hanging around the bar and the nearby beach. I vaguely recall we're somewhere near the Westin Resort, a nice-looking place that wasn't on my list.

"What do you want?" I ask Taylor over the music, and her wandering eyes suggest she's looking for something other than what's on the menu.

She orders a margarita, and I get a mojito and an order of French fries. It feels good to relax and be in a place where everyone is carefree.

My mood dims only slightly when "Single Ladies" by Beyoncé comes on. Is there nowhere on Earth I can go to escape her?

We enjoy our drinks and spend some time mingling with guys and some small groups, but nothing clicks, and the magic doesn't seem to be happening for either of us. It's fine, since I still have my heart set on Miles and know there are more important ways I'll be spending my evening tonight.

I sigh, thinking back to Alice and how this all started. Even if my parents had lost their fortune, they still hadn't been held responsible for what they'd done to me, to all of us, and they had to do something to get my sister out of prison.

It seemed likely that they'd need to be offered something in order to assist, but I don't know what I could possibly give them if their money and freedom were going to be stripped away. I'll have to figure it out fast.

Leaning over, I nudge Taylor with my elbow. Surprisingly, she now appears comfortable hanging out with me near some tiki torches, not ravenously latching on to any guys who stroll by.

"Before it gets too late, I need to go talk to my parents to try to get them to help my sister. If they know the jig is up, maybe they'll be willing to do something for her," I say.

Taylor raises a stylish black eyebrow, as if she doesn't believe me. She sips from her straw and shrugs.

With a response like that, the next logical thing would be to get going then, but I hadn't exactly expected to get moving right away, and some trepidation sets in. The Ritz-Carlton appears to be a ways down the beach, and a stroll along the secluded sand beside some vegetation bordering sounds nice, if isolated.

Swallowing my reluctance, I nod to Taylor and set off, only for her to leave her half-finished drink behind at the table and start walking with me, unasked. I chuckle to myself. All I'd wanted in Hochatown was to make a friend, and somehow I may have actually done it.

"What's so funny?" Taylor asks, dragging her sandals a bit in the sand.

Put on the spot, I take a deep breath.

"Oh, nothing. I'm imagining what would've happened if the way we are now is how things were between us when we set off for Hochatown during Labor Day weekend," I say, smirking.

Taylor casts a furtive glance at me.

"Even without knowing what Alice had in mind, I would've told you to run for your life," she says.

We take a few more steps along the lengthy beach, some

sparse clouds and the stars above us. The water has settled down, gently lapping at the sand, which makes it all the more noticeable when there's some slight rustling in the bushes around the palm trees to our right.

We're a ways from the bar and not close to the next resort, the beach entirely to ourselves.

Taylor doesn't seem to notice it, but I eye the greenery carefully, a strange sensation coming over me. I catch a glimpse of something, faint but unmistakable, especially after all of the practice I've had.

Someone is watching us.

Shaking my head, I keep staring but come to a gradual stop. *I should've known he wouldn't be able to stay away for long*, I think.

I give Taylor a knowing glance before I call out, "Alright, you can come out and stop being such a creeper, Wesley!"

As I think how we'll deal with him crawling back after running away, the bushes and ferns nearby shift more dramatically. It's dark, and a figure bursts out onto the beach at us, large and menacing.

Before I can even scream, he's reached us.

It's not Wesley.

26

A hand clamps hard over my mouth, and I'm pulled off my feet as someone takes hold of me. At the same time, I notice another figure emerge from the bushes as well, shorter and thicker than the first, subduing Taylor easily.

Even though it's dark and I can't see their faces, an uncomfortable sensation hits me that this isn't a random attack.

No, these are my parents' FBI-pretending henchmen, and the realization calls to mind all sorts of terrifying implications.

Our struggles don't last long, some kicks, twists, and thrashing, before both of us are held tight, worn out, and beaten up enough that we can't resist when they pull us back into the bushes from whence they came.

It's disheartening to think that I'd fought so many times and held my own only for someone to commandeer me so quickly and easily, but I had nothing to fight back with and was barely able to make a peep.

Our heels make trails in the sand as we're pulled away from the beach.

I cast a worried look at Taylor, who is still twitching frantically but without much force behind it. No doubt she has a few thoughts about why a couple of guys would capture a couple of girls on the beach, but I doubt she has any idea what we're really in store for.

The questions are too many to count. Have these guys been here watching us the entire time without us knowing? Do my parents already know they've lost the money? If so, these two thugs—the one tall and inked up, while the other's got burn marks and a busted-up nose—might simply dispose of us as soon as possible.

Even though it's a small island, I have no doubt there are places where our bodies could be hidden for a good long while.

Mostly, I'm wondering if my parents had hinted that these two were coming with them. Had Mom mentioned it and I'd forgotten in the whirlwind of everything that happened in their office?

As we breach the other side of the bushes onto a secluded stretch of sidewalk between resorts, I see a dark-gray van parked by the side of the road with a rental company logo on the side.

There's no one around, but I do my best to try to wrench my mouth free enough to call for help anyway. Some unintelligible sounds squeak out, but no one's going to hear them or come running for us.

It gets easier to speak when the hand slips off my mouth to yank the van's sliding door open, but I barely have time to yelp as I'm tossed roughly into the middle seat, colliding with the far side of the vehicle.

If that wasn't uncomfortable enough, I feel Taylor when she's flung in after me, colliding with my hip. Inside the van, and with loud music playing elsewhere, shouting at the top of my lungs wouldn't do us any good.

The tall one, handsome with short dark hair and tattoos on his neck, climbs in behind us. The shorter one slides into the driver's seat and twists the keys.

"We're going for a ride. If either of 'em move, show 'em what happens," he says in his raspy, thick voice as we manage to sit up.

In between us, the edge of a knife glints in the streetlight. The blade's four or five inches long, and one edge is jagged, a hunting knife of some kind. The taller, silent guy behind us slowly withdraws it out of sight.

Not doubting for a second that they would use it if we caused trouble, I'm inclined to sit tight and go along to wherever they're taking us, but he didn't say anything that would prevent me from using my voice.

"If this is about the money, we don't have it," I say.

I can dream about Miles and Wesley swooping in to save us, but it's probably only a dream since neither of them know where we are, and we're pretty much on the outs with both of them.

It strikes me that this might be a ransom play to get their money back, if my parents found out it was missing. Would Miles give back the money to get me released? I might be biased about my own self-worth, but even I doubt my life is worth seven hundred and fifty million dollars. And after my last conversation with Miles, I have serious doubts he'd pay even a fraction of that much for me.

No, we're going to have to find a way out of this jam on our own.

The island isn't that big, and the ride doesn't take that long. My first thought is that we'll be taken to The Ritz-Carlton, where we'd have to face my parents, but we instead turn onto another small street somewhere in the middle of town away from the beach.

A dirty, damaged sign reads, "The Tropical Sunrise Resort," though the dilapidated one-story building has a visible lean to it and a roof missing a number of clay tiles.

I cringe as I peer out the window. This is one of those places

I completely rejected as a possibility when trying to find my parents. Although I have some low standards about places where I'd stay in a pinch, this weather-beaten and ill-maintained place is one I'd never voluntarily set foot in. The travel website evidently hadn't been informed that this place had shut down completely.

But the van comes to a stop at the back of a gravel driveway, where a path leads to the back of the dark structure. It's clear no one else is staying here, and this is the kind of place people will pretend they didn't see if they walk by.

I hear a sound behind me in the back seat, and the next thing I know I feel a piece of duct tape slapped over my mouth. The guy up front turns back to us as his partner tapes Taylor's mouth too.

"We're going to head inside, nice and easy with no quick movements and no noise," he says with an edge to his voice as he leers at us.

Before it was the tall guy with the tendency to ogle, but now the team leader is no better, possibly taking a liking to Taylor.

The van door slides open again, and we're pushed out in reverse order and prodded down an overgrown path between the back of the building and an empty, disgusting pool.

It surprises me when I feel Taylor take my hand, and I remember that I have to be strong and hold it together, or else she could fall apart. If there was a time we could use some of her crazy, it's now, but we'd better wait for a good moment to avoid any unpleasant consequences.

The stockier one pops open the back door of the building and ushers us into a pitch-black room. I bump against a hard piece of furniture, veer to the side, and hit my shin against what seems like a coffee table.

I grit my teeth, trying to fight off the sting, when the lights come on, revealing a dated interior with visible damage from the elements and possibly even animals. My best guess is this is a condemned building that this pair discovered and are going to use to keep us locked away while they make their demands.

My sandals squish against the thin carpet, and the air has a musty quality to it that can't be healthy.

"Let me show you to your room," the man says to us while eyeing Taylor, who has her arms crossed and is shivering.

We leave the central common area and head to one of a few doors on the left side, a bedroom where all of the furniture had been cleared out, except for two frail-looking wooden stools positioned under a bare lightbulb.

I wonder how long they'd been planning this—probably as soon as my parents caught me searching their room, for all I know.

"Take a seat until we're ready for you," the leader says, guiding us into the room and then closing the door after taking Taylor's phone.

Taylor and I are sealed in the empty room, nothing to do but look around at the cracks in the walls, the dingy narrow window, and the bathroom area that had been completely torn out. We help each other take the duct tape off and share sorry looks.

"I wish instead of having these stupid fights we'd flown home this afternoon," I say, pinching the bridge of my nose.

Nervous and with her head lowered, Taylor says, "Why do you think they brought us here?"

I shake my head, knowing I can't have her collapse in on herself in a tough moment like this.

"I don't know, but we're going to get through this. Do you hear me?" She nods meekly. I have to grab her sleeve to shake her out of this. "Taylor?"

"Yes, alright," she says, and I see some fight in her eyes despite a small cut on her cheek.

I open my mouth again, but suddenly the door swings open

behind us, making me swiftly spin around. The two guys step in, grisly looks and menacing eyes.

We only have to somehow make it to tomorrow morning before we can fly out of here. Of course, that involves getting out of captivity and reaching the airport. I keep glancing at the cracks in the walls, imagining having the time and ability to tear a hole big enough for us to crawl through, but it seems unlikely.

Since these guys work for my parents, I have a feeling our ticket home goes through them, but I have no idea how furious they are or what they'll do with all of their money gone. I have to come up with a way to twist the situation to my advantage.

The shorter of the two, the one with the broken nose who'd posed as an FBI agent when he interviewed me days ago, glances back and forth between the two of us.

"Why the long face?" he asks Taylor mockingly, and she glares at him, arms crossed.

"Why do you think? You guys are scum," she snaps back at him. "What are you going to do with us?"

The guy simpers, scratching the large bicep peeking out from under his sweaty cotton t-shirt. They're both wearing torn jeans, though the taller one has on a tight tank top that reveals his entire tattoo. I'd thought it was a gang symbol, but now I think it's some kind of tribal art. These goons look much more like Dallas street riffraff than they did before with fake uniforms.

"Whatever we want, but lucky for you we don't want much. Go ahead and sit down and stay awhile. We wouldn't want your mom and dad getting upset that we didn't show you the proper hospitality," he says to Taylor.

I squint and then share a quick glance with Taylor, a lot traveling between us as we sit on the stools. My hair color has changed, I've gotten some sun, and the huge bruise that was on my face has vanished pretty much completely.

My guess is neither of these guys spend much time with girls in their early twenties, and they don't know which of us is which.

"My parents?" Taylor asks hesitantly.

Our lead captor clears his throat and then leans closer to her, whispering, "Once their evening spa session is over, they'll be right here, and you'd better hope it's a good one that calmed them down some. They are foaming-at-the-mouth angry, and I wouldn't want to be in your shoes right now."

My breath catches, remembering Mom pulling a gun on me and firing it when she was evidently simply trying to give me a life challenge. Dad's threat looms large in my mind. Yes, I'd completely ignored it, but I didn't think I'd have to face the consequences so quickly. I highly doubt either of them will be merciful, so I have to think of something.

Taylor chokes up, seeming to sense that our outlook is not a good one with no one knowing we're here and my parents' history of abuse. She tilts her head down before bucking up.

"If that's how it's going to be, then fine. Mom and Dad don't want both of us though," Taylor says in a harried voice, glancing at me. "Let her go. Taylor's the smarter and prettier one anyway with a brighter future and more people who love her. She can get out of here, right?"

I narrow my eyes, quickly weighing the ability to escape and get help versus all of those slights.

"Stop, don't sacrifice yourself for me," I say halfheartedly, though begrudgingly I do have to admit that it would be the mark of a true friend to invite some of my parents' wrath.

But the burly guy in front of us shakes his head.

"I don't think so. Your little friend is going to have to stick around, and we'll all get a front-row seat for what happens when somebody double-crosses Mr. and Mrs. Marks."

27

Our talkative captor leaves us alone with the taller, stoic one, who Shelley at Bedrock thought was sexy in a dangerous sort of way. But with the tattoos, angular face, and generally scowling disposition, he pushes the bad boy thing to the extreme and comes off seeming depraved.

My first guess is that he's here to stand guard or make sure we don't try to break the window with the stools to escape, but he keeps watching us too closely and then begins to wander around the small room, eyeing us from different angles.

All Taylor and I can do is cringe and try to ignore him, but after a few minutes he begins breathing heavily. Right around then, I wish the other guy would come back or that my parents would show up, but they don't, and we're stuck sitting uncomfortably as he stalks around the room.

Taylor and I commiserate silently, hoping this will be over soon, when I catch the guy at the corner of my field of vision, sizing us up with a finger on his chin. I know better than to engage him and I try to mentally check out, willing myself to disappear and for time to skip ahead to whatever happens next.

But the seconds and minutes drag.

I've successfully drifted off in my mind, imagining the kind of romantic beach vacation one would expect in this kind of place. One that doesn't involve pushing the guy I like into a terrible situation that causes him to snap and run away. Glumly, I know it was bound to happen. I probably make Miles as uneasy as our creepy captor with the lurid looks makes me.

Blinking, I realize that he's gone and jerk my head, wondering if I'd really spaced out enough for him to leave without my noticing.

That's when I feel his finger brushing against my cheek and down my neck. I recoil and lean away from him, hoping that'll be enough to dissuade him, like his touch that makes my skin crawl is some kind of accident.

No, he keeps going, slipping his fingers through my hair and then dragging his fingertips down my back. Unable to stand it anymore, I have to say something.

"Sorry, do you mind if we have some space to talk?" I say gently, trying not to make him mad.

Even though I'm talking to him, my eyes are on Taylor, whose furrowed brows and disgusted scowl makes it seem like she's even more grossed out than I am.

The guy steps behind both of us, and I see him reach out and begin to massage her shoulder. When he leans forward, his head nearly in between ours, his heavy breathing fills my ears. His eyes are a little bloodshot, which I didn't notice before. He's had at least a couple of drinks, based on the smell of his breath.

"There's nothing we can't all share together," he says in a deep, rumbly voice, the first time I've heard it.

His fingers lightly pinch my earlobe and then tug a little on my shoulder strap. I want to throw up and start to think fast about if the two of us could take him. It would be a roll of the dice, one we might have to take, unless...

"I hear someone coming," I say, tilting my head to the door.

It gets him to stop for exactly one second until he continues to run his finger under the hem of the back of my shirt.

"Nah, that's nothing. This place creaks," he says.

"I heard it too. I think the other guy is coming back," Taylor says, a valiant effort to try to sell him on the idea, but he isn't buying it.

He tugs on her ponytail, forcing her head back a little, enough to make her squeak. Seeing him touch her gets my anger up.

"No, stop. That's enough," I say, clenching my fist at my side.

That amuses him, and then he does it again to Taylor. The next thing I know, he's grabbed some of my hair so he could pull it as well.

"Or else what?" he says, relishing it.

I knew trying to say anything to him was a bad idea, because he's taking it all as an invitation to go further. He wants this to get physical, violent, and I feel like I'm running out of options before this gets to a point where we're not able to fight back.

"I have to go to the bathroom," I say, trying to come up with any way out.

"Liar," he says, and I grit my teeth.

If there's a time and a place to lie, it's now, but nothing I say is going to be enough to get him to leave us alone while we wait for someone else to show up.

His fingers skitter over my shoulder like a spider crawling over to the front of my chest, inching farther down while the rest of him leans against my back.

Bracing myself, I shoot Taylor a last look, what I hope is a signal to shock him with our overwhelming combined force.

A deep breath, a flexed arm, and then I jerk my elbow back as fast and hard as I can, trying to catch him in the side, but he catches my arm and squeezes it tight, a sudden searing jolt running through my appendage.

Taylor tries to turn on him as well, but he catches her by the back of the neck before she's barely able to shift around.

"Ow, let go!" I squeal while Taylor tries to reach back behind her head to rake his arm with her nails.

"I like it rough," he gloats.

He's squeezing my arm so tightly it feels like it'll break. I set my feet on the floor, planning to buck back into him, when the door bursts open.

The three of us freeze as a middle-aged couple comes in, pastel-colored beachwear for her and the Hawaiian shirt and navy-blue swim trunks for him. My parents look distraught and enraged, and I can't tell if it's because of what they've walked in on or how much money they've lost.

My heart skips a beat when I wonder if they might be vindictive enough to tell him to keep going.

"Terrance, get your hands off them!" Dad howls, growing red in the face and stepping forward.

The pressure on my arm ceases immediately, and my dad storms over to take the brooding thug with the dorky-sounding name by the arm.

"You can go find Mickey and get some sleep. It's late," Dad says sorely, pushing Terrance past my mom and out so he can close the door. I wonder if either of those guys realize there's no longer any money to pay them. My guess is they'll be back on the streets of Dallas soon, unless they're stuck here.

Despite the unpleasant scene my parents walked in on, Mom has her arms crossed and a stony look on her face as she appraises the two of us. At least she's not waving a gun around yet, giving me a moment to try to think of something.

This is it, and I have to count it as a good sign that they came when they did and didn't approve of the way we were being treated. Even compared to how they looked earlier today, the bare bulb casts a harsh light on them that makes them seem older, more human.

I have to find a way to make things right while deciding what's fair. Their money is gone, and as they stand there with tense looks it becomes clear that they're not going to outright attack us. Whatever they said in their resort room, it may not have been complete baloney.

But Mom's simmering glare deepens as Taylor draws her attention. I know better than to think she can't tell the two of us apart as we sit here on the pair of wooden stools.

"Your name's not Emily," she grumbles. I can imagine she's kicking herself for not putting it together before Wesley was talking about me.

My unlikely partner in crime investigation perks up, no doubt feeling better now that the thugs are out of our lives.

"I'm Taylor Quince, formerly Bedrock's best accountant," she says with a sly smile.

"When you had Director Ron Zee get Alice Patterson to come kill me, she brought Taylor along. Luckily we managed to figure out what was happening and put together a plan to find those responsible. That would be you," I explain, sitting up with good posture.

Dad still has the incensed look that he had when he was going after Terrance. His anger is still there in full force when he stoops slightly to enter my personal space.

"Emily," he says, his voice low and serious, "I told you not to turn on us."

That's all I need to hear to be sure they're aware that their money is gone. While the threat bothered me before, I don't have any regrets about what I've done and am not so much as going to flinch at hearing it again.

Maintaining a firm look into my dad's dark-brown eyes, more like Melanie's than mine, I slowly say, "You did tell me that, but the money you took didn't belong to you and needed to go back. I'm not sure what you imagined doing to me if I turned against you, but I wouldn't advise it."

Mom puts one hand on her hip, her lips pursed. "And why's that?"

I squint at her, surprised I really need to spell this out.

"Because first of all, if you want to start over with somebody, you don't kidnap them. Secondly, the guy whose hands you put all your money into, Miles, will never give you one dollar of the stolen money back. He also knows your aliases and your room number. You should take a second to consider that out of everybody here, you're the ones in deep trouble, not me."

Mom and Dad share a look that leads Dad to step back and take Mom's hand so that they can glare at me together, except this time for once it's not two versus one. With Taylor next to me, I'm not about to back down.

"Is that a fact?" Mom asks, skeptical. She's used to lying, and while it's true I don't know where Miles is or exactly what he's done, I'm sure he'll listen to me about other things besides the money going back. I've already agreed to that anyway.

"One you can count on," I say, stepping off the stool and standing eye to eye with them. Taylor does the same, and I go on, "So let me give you a proposal. Here's the deal."

Marty Marks raises one eyebrow and crosses his arms, leaning back slightly.

"I'm not sure you're in any position to be proposing deals," he says.

"I think I am," I say quickly and forcefully. "Even if what you said about wanting to bring our family back together is true, the thing you forgot is that nobody gets a second childhood. There's no way to redo parenting or put it off and try to make up for it later. I have to live my own life now, and I want to do it on my terms in a way that can be respected.

The Marks name might not mean much to either of you, but it's the only one I've got. So I think you should hear me out."

I'm not sure I've ever spoken so firmly to my parents before, not emotional and defiant like I did in Mom's office but rather in a mature manner, confident that the upper hand is there for me to take.

Mom regards me carefully. "Go on."

I take a deep breath and then glance at Taylor, gathering strength.

"The investors you stole from will get everything back that they put in. The other Bedrock employees can get as much as they're owed from what's left at the company, and then they'll have to find other jobs. There's no other way around that. The only one left with a grievance is me for what you put me through—well, me and Melanie. And I'm willing to take it on the chin if you'll do what's right for her.

"You have to take responsibility for the nursing home scam you perpetrated that got her sent to prison. One way or another, you have to do something to get her out so that she can live her life too and we can have the girls' time we were always supposed to have. We can make the most of what's left if she doesn't have to spend the next decade behind bars."

"Is that it?" Mom asks, and her snappy reply makes me wonder if she really heard me or thoughtfully considered anything I'd said.

"Yes."

My parents glance at each other, still holding hands and leaning against each other. Between Dad's downcast eyes and Mom's gaze lifted to the ceiling, I don't know what they're looking for, but I can't see them finding much.

"Let me get this straight," Dad says. "We lose all of our money, we lose the company, we lose our extravagant lifestyle, and we lose any future we imagined with you. Do I have that right?"

I bobble my head a little, calculating.

"Pretty much, yeah," I say.

Mom scratches her temple and gives me an incredulous look.

"I don't know how you never learned this, but usually with a deal there's something for both sides. Is there anything we *do* get out of this?" she asks.

"Yes," I say, still struggling to weigh everything they did with what they could do for Melanie. I'm no expert and doubt it stacks up neatly, but my choices are limited too.

Mom's eyes widen when I don't immediately go on.

"Are you going to make us ask what it is?" I can see she's ready to smirk and laugh at me, like I can't figure out what they might really want.

I shake my head and come right out with it.

"I'll let you go free."

28

Instead of laughing at me or dismissing me, my parents hold my gaze, straight-faced but attentive. They're listening.

"You'll be able to go on and live your lives like you should have from the beginning, enjoying each other's company and loving each other. You'll never be able to come home, and you'll have to make up new names, but I won't turn you in or come looking for you. That's if you can get Melanie out of prison," I say, letting it hang with an air of expectation.

They look at each other, communicating silently like they have a telepathic link. Mom's furrowed brows make it clear she's not happy, but Dad appears warmer, more content. I wonder if I have to explain that they'd likely be sent to different prisons if they were arrested. My impression is they'd do anything to stay together.

"Alright," Mom acquiesces, her shoulders dropping, "have it your way, Emily. And for what it's worth, I'm sorry about the things I said in the office. Maybe I'm too smart for my own good and everything I've done has been a mistake."

With no reason left for her to lie, I embrace the sentiment

and accept it, which feels like it's worth more than she might think.

"I appreciate that and am going to do my best to forgive you for what happened to us, but I hope you want to learn from your mistakes. When you're out in the world, don't repeat what happened at Bedrock, the nursing home, the lemonade stand, or any of the other times. Forget about the cheating and the scamming. Just get jobs somewhere and live simple, honest lives."

Dad raises an eyebrow.

"Are you tacking conditions on to a deal once it's already been made? Maybe you really do deserve the Marks name."

He's kidding and is trying to get a rise out of me, but I'm not in a laughing mood yet. Shaking my head, I try to tell him with sympathetic eyes that I'm serious.

"No, it's not a requirement, and I know well enough how hard it is to make someone change when they don't want to, so I hope you'll learn from this and decide you'd rather avoid the problems that go along with this sort of thing in the future."

"We'll see," Mom says noncommittally.

I smile, feeling more optimistic about their chances than even they do.

"You're smart enough not to let this happen again," I say, and Mom purses her lips. I can see her doubting herself the way I have so many times. "And you owe it to each other to keep yourselves out of trouble."

I think of Miles. Even if he's not here and doesn't know where I am and thinks I have too much of a checkered past to be a romantic partner, I hope he appreciates what I'm saying. He was right about striving to live in a respectable way, and I'll always remember him, no matter if things don't work out between us.

Dad glances at Mom again and then turns back to me, nodding gently. "We underestimated you."

Ahh, perhaps Miles was right about that too.

"Then prove it by fulfilling your end of the bargain. There has to be something you can do to help Melanie, someone you can call to talk about this with, maybe."

Hand to her chin, Mom sighs deeply and tilts her head, thinking hard. She closes her eyes, and I get the impression she's closing in on something.

"I have something that can help. There's an email I wrote to our attorney presenting the idea to blame Melanie for the nursing home problem. He's since passed away, but his law office will be able to verify the authenticity of the email at the behest of law enforcement, and that should help Melanie. My understanding is that we're not the only clients he would bend the rules for, and some other complaints are starting to emerge publicly," she explains.

My eyes widen, and I remember the seedy lawyer with the pinstripe suit telling me to hurry through conversations with detectives. He was as much to blame for keeping me in the dark as my parents were. Celebrating someone's death is usually considered in bad taste, but I'm tempted to bend that rule myself on his account.

"Sounds perfect!" I say with unrestrained enthusiasm.

I don't even realize it when I put my hand on Taylor's shoulder and pull her in tight. I'm smiling so hard that my cheeks hurt, and my fingers and arms feel tingly. If this goes as planned, I could actually have my sister back.

"We can go print it out and drop it off at the bank," Dad says with a wink. I'm about to say yes until I stop myself and think.

"Better yet, we'll come with you to your resort and get it right from you," I say.

We're having a happy moment and have overcome so much, but I still won't let them out of my sights until I have what I want.

"OK," Mom agrees, and she's the first to step toward the door and open it.

If she's anxious to get out of this unsafe structure, I don't blame her. Something miraculous happened in the ugliest, most inhospitable place on this island, and I'll be happy to revel in the memory of it from afar.

We can't get out of The Tropical Sunrise Resort deathtrap fast enough, and that leaves the four of us walking down the sidewalk toward The Ritz-Carlton in the middle of the night. The two henchmen and their van are gone, hopefully never to be seen again as they return to their shady lives without their rich patrons.

The wind is blowing lightly, and the stars are twinkling bright. I feel so awestruck that I wonder if I could reach out and touch them. And if not, getting to put my hand on my sister will be just as good.

Taylor and I walk a short distance behind my parents, who stroll with hands held like love-struck teenagers, whispering amusing and benign things in each other's ears that have nothing to do with massive theft, death threats, or disturbing schemes. If they can keep this up and forget about all of that, they might be OK.

We pass a few bars that are still open at this late hour and some other pedestrians but soon enough get to The Ritz-Carlton, where we walk in comfortably as if nothing has happened and it's normal to be handing over evidence in the middle of the night that exonerates a girl in her early twenties from a long prison sentence.

The lobby is brightly lit but quiet as we pass through, and I glance at the staff behind the desk. I wish Sadie were still on so I could wave to her and rub it in, but her shift must've ended long ago. The staff members have blank smiles for us but don't bother us further.

Navigating the resort like they know it backward and forward, my parents turn down one of the hallways that leads to an office room, computer on and printer all set to go.

"I don't think we'll be able to stay here too much longer. Paid through the week, I think," Mom says wistfully, glancing out through the wall of windows at the moonlight reflecting off the ocean.

"There are other nice places," Taylor says.

Mom shifts her head like she'd forgotten Taylor was with us and then struggles to nod haltingly. She's going to be having to make a lot of adjustments with all of this, but even talking with her without feeling like she's lying or has some kind of hidden agenda seems like a huge improvement.

Dad holds the door open for her, and they step inside and let the door swing closed. Taylor and I stand awkwardly in the hall with the floor lights casting a gentle glow.

A couple of minutes pass, long enough to make me second-guess myself. They could be in there calling their goons to come back and get us. Mom could be typing up a phony letter this very moment to pass off as something she'd written years ago. Suddenly panicking, I think that any second I might have to run again or fight again or kill again.

My heart seizing, I lurch for the doorknob only for the door to swing open on its own, nearly causing me to topple over. But my parents are right there, a piece of paper in hand, and I manage to keep my feet under me.

"Hot off the presses," Dad chuckles, handing over the sheet of paper.

I take it in my hands and look closely at the printed message, beginning with the usual email sender and recipient information and date, followed by the message my mother wrote that orchestrated my sister's incarceration, and there was even a response from the lawyer, "Roger that. Let's discuss."

It's not out of the question that this could be made up, but I do recognize the lawyer's name and even his email address. Whether this message is actually verifiable evidence depends on if it exists on the law firm's email server, not the paper I'm holding in my hands.

I could ask them to show me their email account to prove it, but instead I look for the truth about this in my mother's dark-blue eyes. She knows I'm searching her for signs that I'm being fooled again, but I want to be trusted and want to trust her. Behind her eyes, there's pain too, and I believe she knows that doing the right thing now will help alleviate it.

"Alright then," I say. "Thank you."

I fold the piece of paper and tuck it into a pocket. It hits me then that the next thing for Taylor and me to do is leave, and I might be seeing my parents for the last time.

Mom doesn't tear up, but she does clench her jaw to keep firm. Dad looks me over in a way that seems admiring, and I wonder if he sees a younger version of Mom in me. Perhaps I should be horrified by that thought, but I want to let the grievances and the grudges go.

"Tell Melanie why we did this. Maybe one day she won't hold it against us either," Mom says, breathing heavily as we gaze at each other.

"In the future, we might have to ask if we can see you both," Dad says.

It's a sweet thought. They say time heals all wounds, and we'll have to see how much of it is required to patch up this one. I give them a closed-lip smile.

"You'll know what name I'll be going by," I joke, smirking.

Taylor takes a step down the hall, and I feel the tug to go with her. It's late, I'm tired, and I'm afraid dragging this out could lead to things going sideways.

"I know it hasn't seemed like it, but I love you," Mom says, and Dad echoes it.

There's a lot that needs to be held back to come up with a palatable response. I'm not a judge or jury and have made my own mistakes too. If I were in their shoes, I would know what they would want.

"I love you too," I say, hoping one day I'll think of myself as having meant it. "Be good."

Appreciating the irony of a daughter saying this to her parents, they glance at each other and giggle while I set off down the hall after Taylor, who was nice enough to give us this last moment to ourselves.

We leave the resort promptly and set off down the street.

"Back to the bars to pick up where we left off?" I ask Taylor, ready to go with her preference. "Some of those guys weren't bad."

Taylor kicks a small stone down the pavement, and we watch it skitter around until it comes to a stop.

"Some of them were. I think I'm partied out for tonight and can just hit the sack."

I try to hide a sigh of relief. "Me too."

It takes a little while to hike around to our street and our Airbnb, where the bank sign is still up over the front door. It makes me think of Miles and everything he did to help make what we accomplished today happen, and a hope blooms in me that he'll be inside and awake so I can share it with him.

But inside we find the lights off and the place exactly as I'd left it. The door to Miles's room is open enough for me to see that no one's inside, and I try not to let thoughts of what he might be doing bother me. As he so clearly declared in Three Tequila Floor, we're not together, and he can do what he likes. Sparing him my judgment and disappointment is the least I can do for him after everything he did for me.

Although it's late when I get to bed, I feel optimistic in a way I never have. Usually as soon as I close my eyes, I'm haunted by all of the terrible things that I've done, but for right now I can set them aside and think about the future, which still looks incredibly bright.

I wonder how long it'll take to have my sister back and see her without a glass partition between us, and it might be even longer after that before I let her go. In light of her prison training routine, I bet she has a crushing hug.

The twin bed's thick comforter feels cozy and warm, and I drift off feeling content and safe.

But it seems like I've only closed my eyes when a sound awakens me in the night, footsteps in the living room going this way and that. The thumping grates on me until I begin to consider that someone might have broken into our rental, possibly the guy who'd snatched us from the beach and then put his hands on me, Terrance.

Something about the footsteps makes me wonder if our new visitor is drunk, which only heightens my alarm. If it's not the tall creep with the neck tattoos who is now unemployed, I start to imagine it being Wesley, ready to act on his professed desire for me after emptying a few bottles.

Or did I forget to lock the front door and someone completely random came in? A fleeting thought hits me that Wesley might have been lying about what he did that night in Hochatown. Maybe the serial killer Alice met at the bar who tried to choke me to death wasn't really killed and has found me, despite having one eye.

It's a worrying sign when the footsteps get closer until they're right outside my door. When the knob jiggles, I curl up tighter and try to stay quiet, but it's no use. The door swings open, and I'm sure I've been found.

The adrenaline hits, and I feel the impulse to try to burst out from under the covers and fight my way out, but I give in to the vain hope that the person will go away if I act like I'm asleep.

The footsteps are lighter now as the person enters my small room, no doubt standing over me, and I have no choice but to open my eyes and try to see who's here with me in the dark.

I wouldn't expect Taylor to have some kind of issue requiring company, but right now it's the best I can hope for.

Looking out with eyes wide, I still can't see anything on account of the complete darkness, but I hear breathing, which seems loud against the silence.

I'm trying to keep my own breathing in check, even though my heart is trying to burst through my chest.

Suddenly, a hand clutches my shoulder, and I scream.

"Emily!" a voice calls, calm and recognizable.

The next thing I know, a light flicks on, and I can see the person who broke into my room in the dead of night.

It's Miles.

29

Gasping for breath and trying to get myself under control, I gaze out at Miles in shock. He's looking haggard, distraught even, eyes puffy and cheeks red. His hair... Well, his messy hair is always like this.

"What are you doing here?" I ask quickly between breaths.

He blinks hard, either trying to fight off fatigue or making sure I'm still here when he opens his eyes.

"When I came back, you were gone, and I couldn't find you anywhere. I had no way of getting a hold of you, and Taylor didn't reply to anything. Eventually, I started making calls trying to find out if anyone'd seen you. When the police wouldn't do anything right away, I went out looking for you myself. I feel like I've walked around the entire island!" he explains, getting worked up about it.

Listening to him talk about how hard he was trying to find me is soothing. Even if he doesn't come right out and say it, I can read between the lines and see how much he cares. I sit up, the blanket draped over my lap.

"Actually, the fake FBI agents from Dallas dragged Taylor

and me off the beach and took us to a kaput resort." When Miles's eyes widen in alarm, I wave my hands and blurt out quickly, "But it's OK. My parents came, and actually I have the best news you can imagine, even if you won't like all of it. They know the money will be returned to the investors and that they can't fight it, and they've given me proof that my sister was wrongfully convicted."

Miles grins, catching my enthusiasm. I'm deliriously tired, but the thought of having my sister back is better than any dream I could have while asleep.

"And what's the part I won't like?" he asks, raising an eyebrow.

Nodding, I say, "We have to let them go. I'm sure you think they deserve prison time, and of course they do, but this was going to be the only way they'd help my sister. Maybe it'll make you feel better to know that I told them to turn over a new leaf and make an honest living. If they don't, they'll end up getting caught and jailed anyway."

Miles turns his head and releases a deep breath through his nose. I know he thinks they got off easy, but this is the way it has to be.

"And you're OK with it?" he asks, watching me out of the corner of his eye.

"Yeah, they wanted me to come with them and live my life on the run under another name, but I told them I didn't want that for myself. I want a life I can be proud of that people can respect. Maybe you think that's already a lost cause, but I'll do my best regardless."

He turns back to me, glancing at me sheepishly at first until we lock eyes firmly. I feel his hand settle on my covered knee.

"I had some time to think about what happened and what you said. I don't think I gave you enough credit or listened to you as deeply as I should have. It's not fair for me to fault you for the things you've done when I've done bad things myself, albeit a little further in the past. Your heart is in the right place, and I like that about you," he says.

My lips part in surprise, never having thought I'd hear that from him. As much as I want to go with it, because of everything I've learned I know I have to test him on it right away.

I set my hand over his.

"But you should know that I'm bound to make more mistakes and not live up to my own standards from time to time. And do you know what? I'm going to forgive myself and move on, because I don't think perfection is a realistic expectation of anyone," I say.

Shaking his head slightly, Miles tips onto the bed and sits beside me. His presence is filling me with hope.

"One lie is worth three-quarters of a billion dollars, and maybe two wrongful freedoms are worth one wrongful imprisonment too. But do you know what, Emily?"

"What?" I say reflexively.

"If you'd asked me a week ago if there was anything that would be worth it if it meant compromising my principles, I would've said no. But I've helped a lot of victims, including your sister, and maybe I've helped myself too. But mostly I feel like I've met an incredible person whose perseverance and resilience has opened my eyes to a side of the world I never knew about. And it doesn't hurt that you're beautiful too," he says, looking me over.

I fail to hold back a grin.

"You're not so bad yourself. Your idealism is just what I needed."

I get sucked into my own little world thinking about how nice it is to have someone who makes me want to be a better person when I feel the soft press of fingertips against my cheek.

Miles tilts my head to the side, and he's right there with soft lips and warm breath.

The surprise kiss after I thought I'd lost Miles makes me smile, which makes it even harder to keep kissing with my mouth trying to do two things at once. But somehow I'm able to get my lips under control enough to give him the kind of long, deep, slow kiss that makes my toes curl.

His hand slips to the back of my head into my hair, and with my sleepy eyes closed all I can do is get swept away in the waves of feeling. Between this conversation and the closeness we're sharing right now, I can tell we're building something between us that could grow strong and last a long time.

With how worn out I am, it's a short hop to falling asleep and finally letting go of a day that had so much at stake but paid off big in the end. I'm not even sure exactly when I fell asleep or Miles left, but I may have passed out as abruptly as I did on his couch.

Hopefully it wasn't mid-kiss, because I don't think he'd take that well.

But the morning and my return to consciousness come all too soon, and with our flight coming up I don't have any ability to blow it off and stay in bed. It's miraculous that we don't have to change our flight time anyway, and with how little I brought with me, the silver lining is that getting ready to go is a snap.

Along with Miles and Taylor, I get my things together before we set out for the airport, leaving behind our Airbnb and the host we never met. Miles dutifully removes all of the fake bank paraphernalia and even goes so far as to throw all of Wesley's remaining stuff into a bag and leave it by the entrance.

Whether Wesley comes to get it or not isn't our problem, but it does feel a bit strange leaving the island as three when we came here as four. All the way through security and waiting at the gate for our flight to board, I keep imagining that he'll pop up to take advantage of the free ride, but he's nowhere to be found as the three of us take our seats.

"Having some room to stretch out is great," Taylor says, sprawling over onto a second seat until the same frizzy-haired flight attendant who gave Wesley the champagne tells us to fasten our safety belts.

Although I don't have an empty seat next to me to spill all over, I make liberal use of Miles's shoulder and side, cuddling up and getting comfortable while we wait for takeoff alongside other tanned and well-vacationed passengers retreating from paradise for the hustle and bustle of Dallas.

"So what are we going to do when we get back?" Miles asks, and I turn my head enough to look up at him.

"You mean besides springing my sister out of the women's prison in Gatesville?" I ask, wondering how long it'll take from when I'm able to deliver the letter my parents gave me to the police and when she's able to go free.

I know she won't be out overnight and suppose the best I can hope for is that the justice system will cut her loose over a couple of weeks. Patting my pocket where I'm keeping the printed email as close as possible, I pray that its magic works quickly. Melanie needs her life back, and I need her in mine stat.

"Yes, I do mean besides that," Miles goes on. "None of us has jobs, my bank account is a lot lighter after paying for this trip and returning the stolen money, and I'm going to need to find some way to keep paying my rent."

I sit up and give him a quizzical look.

"I thought paying rent was optional. Give it a try and you'll see that it's debatable how much of a requirement that is," I say, and he smirks at me.

Taylor taps her nails against her armrest.

"Maybe this sounds strange, but I'm really psyched that we

were able to save all of the people who could've lost everything with Bedrock," she says.

"Yes!" Miles cheers.

"Seriously though, this might actually draw some attention. We might hear from reporters or journalists because of this. It would be nice to be noticed for something like this. Who knew that helping other people could actually feel good?"

Narrowing my eyes, I start thinking that over until something occurs to me.

"It might be good for us too. What if we actually tried to keep doing this? There are people out there getting scammed and ripped off every day, and we could try to save people from becoming victims or help those who've suffered losses."

Miles scratches his chin, eyeing me carefully.

"You mean like creating a nonprofit?"

I hadn't thought that far ahead, but it seems to fit.

"Even people who work at nonprofits get paid," I say, lifting a shoulder. "Between your fraud-busting background, Taylor's accounting skills, and my experience with the shady side of Dallas, we could make a big difference."

Taylor chews on her tongue and slides back in her seat.

"I'm in," she says.

"Me too," Miles agrees, taking my hand and giving it a squeeze. "Is this really what you want to do?"

I see the questioning look in his eyes, and I feel the pressure to put my money where my mouth is and live up to what I said about being honest and taking responsibility, but if that's the case then there's a big conflict looming. As much as I want to close this chapter of my life and move on to the next one, I know I can't do that yet.

"I want to if I can, but although my parents and Melanie have been taken care of, there's still one part of this that's not over and can't simply be swept under the rug amid all this success and happy talk. If I'm going to be more responsible, that means taking ownership for what I've done. There's something I have to do first."

I look into his dark-brown eyes and wonder if I'll have to lose everything I've gained as soon as I've gotten it.

The plane takes off into a clear blue sky, but for me there's a big black cloud on the horizon.

30

It feels like I've walked off the plane and gotten directly into Miles's car as we take another driving trip, but there were a few hours in between. I had immediately brought copies of my parents' letter to the Dallas police and an attorney listed as representing my sister and had to trust they'd take it from there in terms of vacating her conviction.

After that, I barely had time to change into clean clothes and say goodbye to Taylor before I asked Miles for another huge favor. Except there's no way he can help me as much as he did tracking down my parents. This is one I'm going to have to do all on my own.

And now we're riding north on Interstate 30 E toward Oklahoma toward a reckoning that has been a long time coming.

We're mostly silent in the car, feelings filling the interior instead of our voices. I watch the arid land transition into forest as we pass over hills and around turns.

Miles keeps glancing at me out of the corner of his eye. I wish he were checking me out, but I know what's really on his mind.

"Are you sure you're going to be alright?" he asks, and I squint at him.

"I can't believe you're asking me that. I'm doing the right thing...for once in my life," I say.

He breathes deeply and releases a ragged sigh as he grips the steering wheel. I'm clasping my hands in my lap, trying to keep my nerves from sliding into dread.

"I'm not saying you shouldn't, but I—"

Impulsively, I reach out and grab his thigh, stopping him cold. Although my smile is forced and mainly for his benefit, I don't have any regrets or misgivings about this.

"I'm not afraid, Miles, if that's what you're getting at."

His eyes widen at me like he's been caught doing something he shouldn't.

"I didn't say you were, but I know this must be tough. It's not like Taylor's doing it as well."

I sigh and settle back in my seat, shifting my head enough to look at the way his hair curls around his ear and the gentle slope of his nose. These are things I'm likely to miss and have to enjoy while I can.

"And if this were last week, I wouldn't be here either, but now it feels like what I have to do. I never want to run from who I am or lie about myself again, and that means starting to accept the consequences. And Taylor's not here because it wasn't her fault. That was just my made-up justification to avoid taking responsibility."

It feels like a long time since I first came this way along the road to Hochatown, but really it was only about a week and a half ago. Every step of the way I thought my life was falling apart irreparably, but I kept going and kept fighting, and the decisions where I stood up for myself and held myself accountable stand out as the best ones I've made.

But most of them didn't carry as much risk as this. Interstate

30 leads to Route 24 then Route 37, and we cross into Oklahoma, the state line like a point of no return where the decision has been made and there's nothing to do but see what happens to me.

It's the middle of the afternoon by the time we reach Idabel. Thankfully we don't need to go all the way to Hochatown or beyond to get to the McCurtain County Sheriff's Office, a bland two-story brick building with a flag flying out front and plenty of parking.

As Miles comes to a stop in the middle of the empty parking lot, all the space around singles me out and makes this seem like more of a foolish decision than I thought. No one would ever come here or do this. Then again, no one had done what I did either.

We step outside of the car, and I feel the gusty wind blow through my hair as I watch Miles rise from the other side of his vehicle. He gives me a long, somber look, but I don't want his pity.

"I'll find a lawyer for you," he says.

I chew my cheek. Where I come from, lawyers are for people who have money, and I'm certainly not in that boat. But I see him trying to sympathize and offer his support, and I think that's the only thing that matters right now.

"That sounds like the kind of thing a guy would do for his girlfriend," I say, hoping to get a smile out of him while in an oblique way suggesting he shouldn't trouble himself.

"You are," he says.

That draws my attention enough to warrant some close scrutiny. I know he means it but can't help seeing some grim humor in it for both our sakes. For me, it figures that he'd come around at the worst possible time. And for him, well, we'll see how much he enjoys being in a relationship with a chick who's just turned herself in.

While we're maintaining eye contact, I nod once deliberately, and that is that. Nothing says off-the-charts romance like pledging ourselves to each other in the face of the ominous justice system, but considering I was being arrested during our first kiss, maybe it makes sense.

I start off across the parking lot toward the office's front door, and Miles joins me for the walk. If the building had been one hundred miles away, I would've been fine to hike it with him, but we get there in a blink, and it's time to say goodbye.

I give my boyfriend a peck with my dry, quivering lips, force a tepid smile and a faint wave, and then step inside.

The bright lights stun me, but eventually I stagger over to the nearest desk, where an older woman with a lot of hair is typing something on a keyboard. When she sees me coming, she stops and gives me a strange look.

"I'm here to see the sheriff," I say.

She purses her lips, points to some seats by the entryway, and gets up to head through the room and out of view. I don't sit down, afraid I won't be able to rise again, and instead lean against a nearby chest-high counter. There are a handful of people at desks throughout the office area, deputies or whoever else works in a place like this.

The lady at the desk doesn't return, but a burly guy with a thick mustache does. In his mid-forties with the tan-colored uniform, I recognize the man who revived me at the lake immediately. I'd never gotten his name.

I would've expected him to break into a run to tackle me to the floor and grab me, but he takes his time coming over.

"Can I help you?" he asks, and I wonder if he's not recognizing me because of my hair color. More likely he's simply relaxed and comfortable here and is forcing me to talk first.

"I'm Emily Marks. I'm turning myself in for the death of Alice Patterson."

Although he grows serious, and I can see I have his attention, he still doesn't react as much as I'd imagined he would. No popping eyes or gaping mouth now that the fly he's been trying to catch has jumped into his web.

His eyebrow slowly rises.

"Turning yourself in? Are you admitting guilt?"

His even keel is helping me stay steady. If this is routine police work for him, perhaps I can trick myself into treating this like a normal conversation.

"No, but I am involved, and you already know that. I'll tell you what happened, and I'll also give you this," I say, slipping my fingers into my pocket and producing a small slip of paper.

After I set it on the counter, the sheriff picks it up and squints at it.

"What is this?" he asks, grimacing at me.

I plainly explain, "This check made out to Alice is payment for her murdering me, which she was instructed to do by our employer, Bedrock Financial. Director Ron Zee gave this to me when I returned the next day posing as Alice, which I had to do to try to ensure my safety while trying to figure out what was going on there. Needless to say, the attack Alice initiated against me in pursuit of this check resulted in her own death."

That gets the shocked expression I was looking for, and it appears the sheriff stares through me while his brain reboots after hearing that. I stand there placidly while he rubs his face and sets more of his weight against the counter.

"Let's have you come in and take a seat. You're going to be here for a while," he says not unkindly while signaling to one of the deputies in the room to come over.

"I figured," I mutter.

They take me to a small conference room with a table, and this one has a window too, which makes me feel less trapped even if there's not much to look at outside.

It takes them a while to get ready to grill me, but when they start they don't need to ask many questions. The whole story comes out from beginning to end. The only thing I leave out is the identity of my parents, although I still explain that the company owners were worried that I would discover the truth about their Q Fund scam.

"And out of a company of four hundred employees, why were they so worried you alone would figure this out that they wanted someone to kill you?" the young and nerdy deputy asks, hunched over the table with eyes narrowed.

"It's because of my dogged resilience, keen observational skills, and all-around brilliance," I say, smiling with clasped hands over one knee that's crossed over the other.

Both the sheriff and the deputy look at me carefully and then continue going over what I've said until they leave me alone in the room again.

What they believe or what they'll do or what'll happen to me are all completely out of my hands, and I've come to peace with it. I regret my involvement to the extent that others ended up getting hurt, but I don't regret defending myself and trying to keep myself alive.

Eventually the sheriff comes back in, alone and expressionless. I gaze at him blankly, not feeling the need to say much more of anything after exhaustively sharing my story.

"We're going to be taking you into custody. As of right now, you're under arrest," he says.

So that is how it's going to be. I suppose I never expected anything different, but I still held out hope that somehow I'd catch a lucky break.

"Do you have an orange jumpsuit for me?" I ask, thinking of Melanie and how I'll be going in right as she's coming out.

The sheriff cracks up and shakes his head.

"For now, you can wear your own clothes."

He takes me to a holding cell, one of a handful in a large, sterile room. There's a cot with a blue blanket and a short concrete wall that partially separates a toilet from the rest of the space. Someone else is in the farthest cell, but otherwise it's only me.

Taking a seat on the cot, I watch them swing the cell door shut and lock me in. Lost time without my freedom grows from minutes to hours to days. The promise that I can keep my clothes doesn't last for long, though my jumpsuit is dark blue and makes me look like a blob.

Mostly I'm resigned to it and try to keep a positive attitude. This may be my life now, boredom and following orders. The exercise facility leaves something to be desired, so I don't foresee myself getting jacked like Melanie. I do spend time reading things I never would have otherwise.

Things happen fast and slow at the same time. There's the waiting, but then there's also meetings and phone calls with the lawyer Miles got me. Some girls get dinners out, flowers, or jewelry from their boyfriends. I get treated to legal assistance.

The lawyer, a smart lady in her thirties who has never had to spend a day in my shoes, tells me that we'll have to fight hard for a self-defense argument, since the check doesn't explicitly state that it's payment for a murder. My parents are far from the only Bedrock executives who've attempted to vanish, so there's no one around to confess their involvement.

My arraignment comes, and I'm marched into a courtroom where a judge reads the charges to me and asks me how I plead.

"Not guilty," I say, although admittedly it took me some time to really wrap my head around how I could do something and not be guilty of doing it because of the reason why I did it. The last thing I'd want to do is lie to a judge, especially after swearing an oath.

After that, it's back to my cold, lifeless cell and the task of preparing for my trial. I don't know how much time Miles's lawyer is putting into this case or how much she charges per hour, but both have to be a lot.

Two weeks pass, and it feels like the longest stretch of time in my life. I can't imagine how Melanie has survived years of this.

I manage to get to have a call with Miles the day before the trial begins, and he sounds much more optimistic than I'm feeling or that I would've expected. Whoever the twelve jurors will be, I hope they see I didn't want any of this. Miles remains upbeat for my sake, and I try to set my trepidation aside and embrace it.

The holding cell doors open on the day my trial is set to begin, and I glance at the clock despite having just done so and confirm that they're here a full hour early to get me.

I grit my teeth, preferring to be alone than spend that extra time waiting for people to show up to dissect the things I've done.

My lawyer walks in first, nearly six feet tall in a light-gray blazer and tight skirt, looking like she owns the world. But behind her is Miles, and I immediately get to my feet and walk over to grasp the bars.

"What are you doing here?" I ask with a smile at seeing him in a t-shirt and jeans. "Isn't that a little casual for court?"

I figured he would've been back in the audience somewhere, if he didn't finally decide that this relationship wasn't right for him.

But Miles casts a sly smile at my lawyer, who brushes some long red hair away from her face and wields a leather-bound folder.

"It would be," Miles answers, "but I'm not going to court."

It's harder to maintain my smile after that, but I try not to show that I'm devastated. With all of this, Miles has been my rock, my only leg to stand on. It crosses my mind that my lawyer might have a bit of a cougar in her, going after the recent college grads.

I stammer, "Oh, I...can't blame you. I doubt it'll be fun."

Miles chuckles and stuffs his hands in his pockets, leaning back.

"So what should we do instead?" he asks.

"What?" I say reflexively, trying not to take offense. I won't be doing anything else other than sitting through my murder trial.

Miles doesn't clear up what he means, and eventually my lawyer unzips her folder.

"If I may," says my lawyer, Alexandria, "this might help."

She hands over a printed sheet of paper that I find myself having trouble reading in my current emotional state. I can barely make out my own name, the one I thought was so important to fight for and keep that I'd go through all of this for it.

"What is this?" I ask, lost.

Miles steps closer and sets one hand over my knuckles, his dark-brown eyes right in front of me while I surely look like a troll living under a bridge.

"The district attorney has decided not to prosecute your case. You're free to go."

The bars keeping me in are suddenly supporting my weight when I collapse against them, wiping my watering eyes with my sleeve.

"Really?" I ask.

Alexandria waves over one of the deputies with the keys.

"They get it. There's no contest," she explained. "It's over, and you're in the clear to put this behind you. The Bedrock situation has gotten a lot of public attention, and even besides the facts it would look bad to go after you."

As much as I would've enjoyed having the McCurtain

County sheriff let me out, I don't particularly mind that it's some deputy I've never spoken to who only knows me from in here.

The door swings open, and I step out like I've crossed over into a strange new world. But Miles is there, and I spread my arms to spill against him next, laughing and crying and smiling and nose running all at the same time.

When I'm finally able to keep my feet under me, Miles shoots me a sharp look with one eyebrow raised.

"So let me ask again. Rather than go to court, what should we do instead?"

I'm still in so much disbelief that I'm barely able to answer.

"Whatever you want," I say, the whole world suddenly open to me. And whatever might be on his mind, I know I'm ten times as eager.

Miles tilts his head and shrugs, tapping his foot and thinking it over as he overdramatizes every motion.

"I know you've probably been cramped in there, but how about we take a car trip?" he asks.

"Sure, where to?"

Miles takes a deep breath.

"I think it'd be a good time to visit the women's prison in Gatesville."

31

B arely taking enough time to get my clothes back and change, I flee the sheriff's office and spill into Miles's car. It's a cloudy morning not much different from when I left, the world acting like no time at all has passed despite weeks of my time vanishing.

It's a surreal feeling being out here in the big world and the wide open spaces of Texas after being cooped up in such a bland environment.

I set five fingertips on the window and marvel at the scenery going by. Even on an overcast day, it's still so full of color. All of the sensory input makes me feel like I'm high.

"So how was it in there?" Miles asks casually, making conversation with one hand on the wheel.

I glance at him out of the corner of my eye, still in disbelief that he's here next to me.

"Not as nice as some other places I've stayed recently. There wasn't much of a view, but I don't think it would double very well as a bank," I say, making him crack a grin.

"The hosts must have been better though."

I shake my head. "At least I did see them, but most of the time I wished I didn't."

He looks me over with lips pursed, and I can see he's holding something back. I'm about to ask him what when he veers to pass another car, probably not the best moment to demand his attention. When he gets us back into the right lane, he casts his eyes at me again.

"The district attorney's decision isn't the only thing that's been going on," he says.

I blink, trying not to let my anxiety resurface. I thought this was all finished and I was in the clear.

"Really? What's left? I thought it took care of everything that happened," I gush.

"Whoa, easy," he says, holding out a hand toward me. "The past did get straightened out, but not the future."

"The future?"

"What we're going to do. I've been working with Taylor to put the fraud-and-scam-fighting nonprofit together like we talked about," he explains, his enthusiasm growing.

I hold back a smile and take a long look over at him.

"Have you really?" I say, having half expected that to be something that got brought up on the plane and then forgotten about, like the food or in-flight entertainment. Or maybe it completely slipped my mind with the whole going-to-jail thing.

He's beaming, and despite the clouds it feels like an incredibly bright day.

"Yeah, it's more or less all ready to go. I've been working on the website and putting together a draft of the mission, all of which you'll be able to review for your approval, but that's not even the best part."

My eyes widen. "What could be better than having someone talented like you put this all together without me having to lift a finger?"

"Heh," Miles snickers, "the part with your heavy lifting is coming up, but you'll have plenty of support. Get this, the Bedrock victims caught wind of what we're doing and put together a contribution out of the recovered funds to get us started. It's not three-quarters of a billion dollars, but it'll allow us to make a real run at this."

If I was surprised before, I'm gobsmacked now. These people have just gotten their money back, and now they want to simply give some of it away again?

"I can't believe it. Really? Are you pulling my leg?"

"Nope."

"OK, how much? Like a few hundred dollars?" I start thinking we could get a desk or maybe a new cell phone after having three lost or broken over the past several weeks.

"Emily, they've put in a million dollars."

"They…" A whooshing feeling hits me that leaves me sprawling against the seat. It's a good thing this car door is locked, or I would've spilled out. Miles's serious tone leaves no room for doubt, and I shake my head and try to grapple with the reality of that much money. "I suppose we'd better be careful about how we manage the funds given to a charity combating fraud!"

Miles nods emphatically.

"We've got that all taken care of. There's going to be a board composed of some of the donors, and of course I'll be keeping track as well, but the need for accountability shouldn't at all stop us from taking on the legitimate expenses of pursuing our mission. In truth, working their generous contribution out with them was the easy part, and not everything has been so smooth."

My hand to my forehead, I'm still reeling at what this means. I'm able to pursue something I care about that I think I can do to make a positive difference. This sounds even better than being a financial planner, and I know I can use what I know, learn more, and be good at saving people from this kind of horrible thing.

Somewhere within my jumble of thoughts, I get back to what Miles said.

"If getting that much money was the easy part, what was hard?" I ask.

Miles sneaks a glance at me and rubs his chin.

Shrugging one shoulder, he says, "To create the nonprofit entity, I had to go ahead and pick a name."

My attention piqued, I focus on him closely.

"And what did you pick?" I ask, trying not to sound tense about it. He'd better tell me quickly before I start to get anxious about not getting to choose the name for the idea I had.

"Like I said, it was hard to land on something that would be quite right. I went through a lot of different ideas. Taylor even came up with some too. We needed something with—"

"Miles!"

"OK," he says, taking a deep breath. "We're calling it Emily's Marks."

Sputtering laughter, I drop my face in my hands and soak it in. Alright then, there'll really be no more pretending I'm somebody else or going on the run now.

Blushing, I reach out and set my hand on his thigh.

"I guess I'd better go through with it since it's basically named after me. We can give EMILYs List a run for its money. I hope I do it justice," I say.

Miles glances at my hand on his leg and then over at me. The way he's looking at me makes me feel warm.

"You're going to do great."

My hand is still on his leg, and I feel like we're hitting a vibe that's both sweet and tender.

"*We're* going to do great," I say, correcting him with a smile.

He tips his head back and raises a finger.

"Oh, there's one other thing. We've got an office too. It turns out there's suddenly a lot of vacant commercial space in downtown Dallas that was going cheap."

I snort, catching his meaning.

"Out of the ashes of Bedrock Financial comes Emily's Marks. I hope it's not on the fourth floor around the human resources department."

"Why's that?" he asks, and I think back to the broken glass, spilled liquor, smashed computer equipment, and huge mess I made.

"No reason."

The road continues to stretch out in front of us as we zip along Texas's highways. The sight of Dallas as we sail by makes me happy, but the promise of what's ahead in Gatesville is even more tantalizing.

With hours more to our journey, I have plenty of time to zone out and imagine every possible way this could play out and how I'll react. Maybe I am turning into a softie, but I already feel like the handles are loosening and my waterworks are going to be on full blast.

But a deeper part of me has some misgivings about what'll happen. It was one thing meeting Melanie behind glass and squeaking through an uncomfortable but important conversation. It'll be another when she's living and breathing around me, where we might really see whether we get along and actually want to be in each other's lives now that we're not kids.

My parents wanted a second chance with us but didn't get it, but Melanie and I are going to have to go through getting reacquainted with each other and building a relationship from scratch. I welcome the prospect of putting in the work and bending over backward to smooth her transition back to her life, but only time will tell how successful I am.

When we arrive at Linda Woodman State Jail in Gatesville,

I'm immediately dispelled of any notion that what I went through was even close to what she'd endured for years. Compared to the county sheriff's office, this place is a desolate fortress in the desert that looks inhospitable and soul crushing.

The car comes to a stop in the parking lot, and I give Miles a sheepish look and quick thanks before climbing out.

To my surprise, he stays right where he is. This guy is too good, even if I'm wearing my heart on my sleeve and wouldn't mind the cover of a third wheel. No, this is the way it needs to be, and the challenge for her will be one hundred times greater than it is for me.

After one last glance back at Miles in the car, I set off for the front doors. Inside, there's a guy behind a check-in counter in front of the security screening area, and I set my elbows on the surface and lean toward the glass.

"I'm here to pick up Melanie Marks."

He nods absently, leans back, and then mutters something into a microphone.

I imagine I'll have to wait a significant period of time for them to dredge her up from deep within the bowels of this imposing edifice, but instead I'm barely able to turn around before one of the interior doors opens.

Out walks Melanie in a gray cotton t-shirt and mid-thigh gym shorts, her sneakers crackling against the floor tiles as she sees me and comes toward me, loose black hair hanging slightly above her shoulders. Whatever this place did to her, it did not diminish her beauty. Those waterworks...

Smirking, she picks up speed and races at me. I can barely take a step or two before we collide, and her hug is exactly as crushing as I'd imagined. My back cracks, and I already know I'll never need a chiropractor. Even though she's my younger sister and is barely in her twenties, she's a fair amount wider than me and heavier, all of it muscle.

The hugging goes on for some time, but eventually I need to breathe.

We look into each other's eyes, but hers drift up to my dyed hair.

"Did you do this for me?" she asks, and I shake my head.

"No, it's a long story. I'll tell you on the ride home. What do you say we get out of here? If you ask me, you've put in enough time in this place."

We glance at the main exit simultaneously, some light filtering in that hints at the outside world. There are some other people around, other visitors and prison workers, but it's Melanie's presence that fills the room.

She shifts her lips to the side as she gives the place a final, dismissive glance. I take a step back to be able to see her as a whole. Not at all broken and beleaguered, she appears confident and poised, so full of life and eagerness. I'm sure what she went through was harrowing and beyond unpleasant, but there may be a kernel of truth in my parents' idea that her difficulties would make her stronger.

Turning back to me, Melanie nudges me with her hip, getting me moving toward the door.

"Let's go. Our time is beginning," she says, striding fast enough that I need to speed walk to catch up.

But it's fine that she's slightly ahead and can't see my greedy grin. I have my sister back. All the lies have been exposed and put to rest. And our future together is sparkling.

And we'll make every day we have together an adventure.

After all, we have a lot of lost girls' time to make up for.

32

"There, it's finished," I say, letting go of the keyboard and leaning back in my seat with an air of satisfaction.

Sitting comfortably in my spiffy leatherback chair in my new office, I take a deep breath and read over my work one final time.

The website for Emily's Marks is ready to go, and we're settling into our new working space as we proceed with our launch and begin to make our presence known in the world. Some helpful journalists did follow up with us after the theft and recovery, and our story will be going live and hitting the news imminently.

My announcement draws the staff. Miles hops out of his chair at a nearby desk to come up beside me and put a hand on my shoulder. Taylor peels herself off a comfy reception couch we have by a bank of windows looking out over the Dallas streetscape.

And Melanie emerges from my old cubicle, since our place in the Bedrock building is the same second-floor area where all of the financial planners were. She's unlikely to be with us forever, and I'm urging her to think about going back to school, but I'm glad to have her close by while she figures things out.

In truth, we're all still figuring things out, full of optimism but also trepidation about the future, which is never certain.

They crowd around me behind my desk as we review the website, reading about our mission, the press we've received, our offerings, and the information we share to help keep people safe, financially and personally. Along with the images and fancy HTML tricks Miles has added, it looks like we run a cool and slick operation.

"This is brilliant," Taylor says.

In a trim beige suit and with lensless glasses, she's been diving into her new role with a level of professionalism and rigor that would make Alexandria the lawyer intimidated.

"You really think so?" I ask, blatantly fishing for more compliments.

"It's perfect. Where'd you learn to write like that?" Miles asks. I set my hand on his hand on my shoulder. Not only has working together been going well, but we've been doing everything together well...and often.

Snickering, I remind myself to be modest. "It's not that amazing, but it came from the heart," I say.

It's a little crazy to think that several weeks ago I was the newest and lowest-ranked person here, and now that company is gone and I'm in charge, albeit in a small portion of the building. I fancy the thought that it could've been like this all along, that I always had it in me, but I know I never would've had the inspiration and drive if I hadn't gone through everything that I did.

I used to think that I had to be better off before I could become a better person, but now I'm committed to doing right and doing well at the same time.

"So what are we supposed to do next, boss?" Melanie asks, sharing cheeky grins with the others, who she's been getting along so well with. Beats the girls in the prison block.

"I keep saying you don't have to call me that!" I say, amused.

"Sorry, what's next, big sis?"

I don't at all mind being called that and join the others as we survey our section of the office in search of other things to do. Empty seats, empty cubicles. Plenty of nice decorations, materials, supplies, and equipment, thanks to our generous donors, but it is definitely missing something.

"I think now we help people," I say and glance at the office's front door and then the phone.

The minutes tick by, and we do the usual things a new startup does. We share our website, send emails to our donors and board members, and check on the news articles that have been written about us.

Everything seems great, but time continues to pass without anybody walking in or reaching out. Nothing comes up that seems to require our assistance.

I exchange smiles with my friends who are now my coworkers, not wanting to hint at a creeping doubt that there may be an issue. I don't for a second think that this is a bad idea, but what if nobody actually needs our help?

I tell myself that it's not possible for thousands of years of scamming and exploitation in the human race to come to an end the minute we open up a charity dedicated to stopping it, but still we're twiddling our thumbs and chitchatting idly. Melanie brought weights to her cubicle and has been getting good use out of them.

Some frustration starts to emerge when I notice a shadow around the closed front door. I peer at it, trying to make sure that I'm not tricking myself into imagining something, when it moves slightly away from a window to the hallway with the elevators.

My first thought is that it's someone from the building doing some work as they transition from one big office to many smaller ones. No, it's not that at all.

Someone is lurking out there and watching me.

Not in the mood for any lookie-loos who've come to gawk when I'm trying to make a difference, I get up from my seat and storm toward the door.

"Phew, the door works," I say, pulling it open and revealing Wesley with shoulders slumped and a hangdog look on his chiseled face. "What are you doing here?"

I'd figured he was gone for good, so to show up here at our office the day we're opening makes me immediately suspicious.

Dressed in khaki shorts and a polo shirt, he looks tired and grim, not with his usual confident swagger or even the despondency he had when I first saw him after Hochatown. He blinks hard. I'd startled him.

"Emily..." he says, and I glance back at the office, knowing that the others are curious about the first person to show up at our door.

I have too much else on my mind that I'm trying to do to get hung up on Wesley's usual nonsense. My first thought is he heard we got some money and is trying to get a piece of it. But despite everything, I'm glad to know he's at least alright and made it back from the island. Even if it didn't work out as planned, he'd helped too to get us here.

An exasperated sigh escapes my lips. "What do you want, Wesley? Do you want a hundred bucks to get dinner or a room somewhere? I can give you that, but then you need to let us go," I say.

Wincing, Wesley raises a hand. "Hey, it's not like that. I'm not here for money. Well, not really."

I roll my eyes and stuff my hand in my pocket. "Right—"

"No, I'm serious. Something happened on the island," he says, shifting to face me, his head listing to the side, the telltale signs of another sob story coming on.

"What?"

"You'll never believe it. After I left, I just partied, but the next night I got a room at another place. I hit it off with this girl and took her back. We were having the time of our lives, but I think she slipped me something in my drink, because before I knew it, I was out cold. When I woke up, I saw she took everything. I was completely cleaned out. I had to beg my parents for a plane ticket back and have been crashing with them since, but I need to get back on my feet."

I look Wesley in the eye, thinking about all the times I've been burned and cheated and tricked. And I take a deep breath and remember that although the shoe is on the other foot, he's the exact type of person who we're trying to help.

Forcing down my misgivings, I smile and step aside to clear the way for him to come inside.

"You've come to the right place. Welcome to Emily's Marks. We offer financial counseling, coordination with law enforcement and banks, and support and planning services," I say.

My spiel attracts further attention from the others, and Miles and Taylor get up from their desks to join me. I feel the tension in the room, plenty of unspoken ire directed at Wesley for a lot of reasons, but everyone still seems ready and willing to help, to their credit.

But after hearing what we can do, Wesley waves it all off and purses his lips. This is uncomfortable for him, but it looks like he's trying.

"I don't want a cash handout, and I think we all know that there are more deserving people than me for this kind of thing you're doing," he says. "I have a better idea."

I cross my arms, already feeling like he's pushing my buttons by pushing his own agenda.

"And?" I say sharply, letting him know he's got one chance.

A fair amount larger than all of us, yet noticeably meek, he casts his eyes over Miles and Taylor.

"I'd like to help. I could spread the word and find people who would benefit from this sort of thing. I know where the people are who are at risk or have already had something happen to them," he says, leaving a lot unsaid. "What if you had someone out there on the front lines to bring people in?"

I open my mouth, completely ready to trash the idea and throw him out, but I manage to stop myself before I make so much as a peep. There are only a few of us, and something like that could actually be helpful. News articles and websites are nice, but we've got to be out there too, where it's happening.

Of course, each of us could do that to some extent, but there would be an advantage in having someone who only did that part of it.

I appraise Miles and Taylor. Although I'm in charge, they have a say too, and the last thing we need is any kind of tension between us with Wesley involved. They chew it over.

"Having someone doing outreach would be nice," Taylor admits, arms crossed as well, and I see Miles nod reluctantly.

"You don't even have to pay me until you know it's working out," Wesley insists.

Holding my breath, I take another long look at him and think about the risk of him representing us, of him re-victimizing people if he tries to take advantage of them. At the same time, this could be the structure and the environment that he needs to live a new kind of life. What if all along the only thing he's needed was a real job?

I extend my hand. "We can try this," I say warily, "but you have—"

"I won't screw this up," he says firmly, and we shake while I've locked on to his blue eyes, letting him know I'm serious.

And surprising us all, Wesley stays true to his word. A week passes, then two, and people keep coming in the door who are both in need and incredibly grateful for everything we can do to help during one of the toughest times in their lives.

Our reputation and our record for making a positive difference grows, and although the job is never done, I leave work each day with Miles sharing attentive looks and soft touches amidst our feelings of satisfaction for what we've accomplished.

Except one day when the clock strikes five but I realize I'm enjoying what I'm doing so much that I don't want to leave.

I look over at Taylor, who's saying goodbye to a client she's been advising, and smile. Miles flexes his fingers after some intense number crunching. And Melanie is getting off the phone with the police, having become a great liaison for victims.

The door opens, and it's Wesley stopping in after a long day of hitting the streets for us. I give him an enthusiastic wave. In slacks and a button-down shirt, he is looking the part.

Feeling warm, I let my attention drift to the objects on my desk, including one picture I have tucked into the corner, an older one but still one of my favorites. I pick up the small frame displaying the image of my sister and me with my parents when we were younger.

While my parents made terrible mistakes, what my experience with Emily's Marks has taught me is that they are human and deserve sympathy, not spite. One day I'm sure our paths will cross again, and that'll be OK, but for now I realize that what I've been really looking for I already have.

Setting the picture down, I pick up my phone.

"Hey, everybody, come over here," I say, leading my sister, boyfriend, and friends over to the plush dark-brown couch by the big windows.

Not needing any direction, we all pile on, crashing together and getting cozy while I hold up the camera and take a new picture that I can't wait to have on my desk as well.

This is my new family, all doing our best to be honest and kind fellow human beings in the glow of the Dallas cityscape and sunset.

Be a Hero and Write a Review!

If you enjoyed *Girls' Time*, please take a moment to write a review for it. Reviews are phenomenally important and are crucial to any book's success. Thank you so much for reading and sharing your thoughts!

ABOUT THE AUTHOR

Jason Letts is the author of over thirty novels, including the bestselling *Agent Nora Wexler Mystery Series* and *Girls' Trilogy*. He's going to keep writing psychological thrillers like these, so get connected to find out when the next story will be released!

To connect and find out about more books, find me at

www.jasonletts.com

https://www.facebook.com/authorjasonletts

Or email me at infinitejuly@gmail.com

Made in the USA
Columbia, SC
16 October 2024

44465686R00133